SAVOR THE UNIQ
YO
"Evocative, moving renditions of p...
—*Kirkus Reviews*

### "BANK NIGHT"

When middle-aged bachelor Pleasant Anderson wins $250 at a Little Butte movie house, he finally gets a date with a redhead . . . or two.

### "THE SKATERS"

From childhood Borghild wanted to marry one of the Ivarson brothers, but she ends up with both in a poignant rural ménage à trois.

### "THE NIGHTS OF RAGNA RUNDHAUG"

A maiden lady living alone with her little white dog "Vittehund" has no desire to become a midwife . . . until she is entangled in a tragedy.

### "BLUE HORSES"

A self-righteous Bible-thumper flaunts his piety to an old friend, who can't resist tweaking his nose with past and present indiscretions.

### "TWILIGHT AND JUNE"

A jilted suitor can't avoid his old sweetheart and her husband, but his final revenge is an act of true love.

Also by Carrie Young
*Nothing to Do but Stay*

# The Wedding Dress

## STORIES FROM THE DAKOTA PLAINS

# Carrie Young

LAUREL

A LAUREL TRADE PAPERBACK
Published by
Dell Publishing
a division of
Bantam Doubleday Dell Publishing Group, Inc.
1540 Broadway
New York, New York 10036

"The Wedding Dress" appeared originally in *Stories* 18 (1987); "Bank Night" appeared originally in the *Yale Review* 74 (1984).

ISBN: 0-440-50524-0

Reprinted by arrangement with University of Iowa Press

Printed in the United States of America

Published simultaneously in Canada

September 1993

10  9  8  7  6  5  4  3  2  1

FFG

FOR MY DAUGHTER

Felicia

Whose enthusiasm and love

encouraged me

every step of the way

# 1

# The Wedding Dress

*I wish I could have known Ildri. I wish that just once* I could have seen her. She was my mother's friend. All during our childhoods, my sisters and brother and I heard these stories about Ildri. How she was the most beautiful woman ever to homestead on the western plains. How—if circumstances had been different—she could have been a governor's wife, or a senator's wife. Ildri, Ildri.

My mother first met Ildri in a dressmaker's shop on Nicollet Avenue in Minneapolis shortly after the turn of the century. Then in her early twenties, my mother had come to the city from a farm in southern Minnesota and had secured a job as a seamstress for a well-to-do dressmaker named Astrid Fjeld. One day in early spring a young woman walked into the shop. She was wearing a black floor-length coat with a high collar and a cinched-in waist that suggested a well-rounded figure underneath. My mother remembered the coat because she had one like it; the leg-o'-mutton sleeves were at that time just beginning to go out of fashion. The woman wore a soft-brimmed black hat under which gleamed an abundance of auburn hair, bouffant in front and wound into a coil in back. She had a round face, an ample round nose, and startlingly white skin, but her eyes were her most striking feature; large and wide apart, they were the color of burgundy and were set so well beneath the brow that they seemed to float in mysterious brown shadows. As the woman walked in, the eyes were luminous and the face mobile as if she would momentarily break into tears. Alarmed, Astrid Fjeld quickly pulled the woman to a chair and asked her what was wrong.

"Nothing is the matter," Ildri had answered somewhat impatiently. "I am looking for work. I am a seamstress."

Astrid Fjeld, an elegant black-haired doyenne who prided herself on her swift intuitive judgment of strangers, began to sputter. "But my dear, you look like you are going to cry!"

Ildri shrugged. "I always look this way," she said.

She was hired on the spot. Astrid Fjeld had just the week before obtained an important order to make the bridal gown for the June wedding of the daughter of one

of the city's flour barons, and she very much needed another seamstress. Ildri, to prove herself, was at once set to
work hand-stitching a petticoat, while my mother and Astrid Fjeld continued on the wedding dress. After an hour
Astrid Fjeld confided to my mother that she was worried
Ildri didn't know what she was about. "All the time she
keeps muttering to herself!"

It was true, my mother said, that Ildri, as she sat sewing,
made small deprecatory remarks such as, "Oh, I'm afraid
Mrs. Fjeld will not find this good enough" and "Poor Mrs.
Fjeld. She will have to rip this up and start over!" When
she had completed the garment, Ildri had tossed it toward
the shopkeeper with a small sigh of discouragement. Astrid Fjeld snatched it up and examined it thoroughly and
then was hard put not to look impressed. The workman-
ship was faultless, the tiny stitches all but invisible. After a
discreet interval, Ildri had joined my mother on the wedding dress and Astrid herself was sewing petticoats.

At the end of the workday, Ildri and my mother put on
their identical going-out-of-style coats and had a good
laugh as they left the shop together. Out on the street,
Ildri confessed she had not yet found anywhere to live,
and my mother at once offered to share her room in a
nearby boardinghouse.

They soon found each other to be kindred souls: they
had been born on the same day. What is more, Ildri's parents, like my mother's, had emigrated from Norway. They
owned a general store in a small town an hour's carriage

ride from Minneapolis. Ildri was an only child, and she and her mother had run a dressmaking business as part of the store. But the mother recently had died, and the father was on the verge of remarrying, so Ildri had decided it was time to go out on her own. She was lonesome. She and my mother sat in their room at night exchanging confidences and speaking happily in Norwegian; although Astrid Fjeld was herself a Norwegian immigrant, she would not allow Norwegian spoken in her shop.

"This is an *Amer-i-kahn* shop," she always declared, heavily rolling her *r*'s. "Here is spoken only *Amer-i-kahn.*"

As the wedding dress began to take shape, Ildri and my mother became more and more excited about it; they began to think it would be the most beautiful wedding gown they would ever see. It was made of white watered silk. It had a close-fitting tucked bodice and a high boned collar trimmed with narrow satin ruching. The skirt had four frills at the bottom; it was straight in front and gathered at the sides and back into a fitted satin waistband. The sleeves were tight-fitting, tucked at the shoulders and frilled at the wrists. A small tulle train floated out from the waistline to the floor. The waist-length veil had ribboned streamers of imported Norwegian Hardanger lace stitched to chiffon.

The bride-to-be came in twice for fittings. A horse-faced woman with drab brown hair parted in the center and pulled tightly into a bun, she climbed impatiently in and

*The Wedding Dress*

out of the gown, neglecting to look at herself in the mirror. She confided to Ildri and my mother that the elaborate wedding was her father's idea; he was a widower and doted on his only child, who—happily for him—had consented to marry the son of the city's other leading flour baron. Her father was also giving her a Victorian house for a wedding gift, and her only interest in that was the stable out back for her riding horses, about which she was wildly enthusiastic. There would be no need to come in for another fitting, she said, noting that Ildri was almost exactly her size and weight and could be her stand-in when the hem was ready to be put in.

One morning as the wedding dress neared completion, Ildri was standing on a low table in the back workroom wearing the gown while my mother and Astrid Fjeld sat on the floor pinning up the hem. The front doorbell tinkled, and before the shopkeeper could get off her knees the bride's father, having seen the door ajar at the rear, appeared in the doorway. Looking every inch the flour baron, he was a florid-faced man with a tremendously protruding stomach across which slithered a diamond-studded watch fob. When he saw Ildri in the wedding gown, a look of intense pain crossed his face, as though something invisible had given him a glancing blow to the midsection.

Startled at his sudden presence in the doorway, Ildri turned so pale that her normally white skin took on the translucence of the wedding gown's watered silk. Her auburn eyes darkened with fright. As she stood trapped on the table, a sunbeam streamed through the high windows and locked her in its web.

The flour baron continued to gaze and then fell into a nearby chair and closed his eyes. "This sight I wish I had never seen," he whispered hoarsely.

Having struggled to her feet, Astrid Fjeld cried, "Sir, you do not like the gown?"

"On the contrary, Madam," the flour baron replied. "It is the most bewitching bridal gown I have ever seen. Tragically, my own daughter will never wear it. Last week she ran off with her stable groom. I have just been informed by wireless"—and here the flour baron let out a terrible groan—"that they have found employment on a horse ranch in Montana."

After taking out a white linen handkerchief and thoroughly mopping his face, the flour baron rose wearily to his feet. "However, Madam," he said, "there is no reason that you should suffer because I spawned a fool for a daughter, so I have come to pay you the full agreed-upon price for the gown. The dress itself you can do with what you will." He pulled a bank draft from his breast pocket and handed it to Astrid Fjeld. Again he gazed for a long moment at Ildri. The sunbeam had moved behind her. She looked suddenly fragile and vulnerable as she bit her lips to keep them from trembling.

Impulsively the flour baron pulled out his wallet. He removed a fifty-dollar bill and pressed it into Astrid Fjeld's hand. "This is for the titian-haired beauty who was born to wear a wedding dress," he said. His eyes fell to my mother who was still kneeling, stunned, at Ildri's feet, a giant pin-cushion in her lap. An almost imperceptible smile softened his face. He pulled out another bill to match the first. "And this is for the snapping-eyed girl." He turned and walked ponderously out of the shop.

Always at this point in her story, my mother would stop and laugh her joyous laugh, and we laughed with her. We all knew what the flour baron had meant by her "snapping" eyes. My mother had intense, glowing black eyes that were constantly changing with her emotions, giving off an infinite variety of sparks that accurately registered her feelings.

◆

In that moment when she had observed the flour baron looking at Ildri, Astrid Fjeld more than likely hatched the scheme that several days later she proposed. She wanted Ildri, dressed in the wedding gown, to sit in the shop's bay window every day at noon for several weeks as a promo-tion for the dressmaking shop. Ildri at first protested that she was much too shy; she would never be able to tolerate being stared at by the pedestrians on Nicollet Avenue for an hour a day. But Astrid Fjeld persisted, finally gaining Ildri's consent by saying she would let her sit with her back turned at a three-quarter-degree angle so that she would actually be looking into the shop and only a small portion of her face would be visible.

Shortly before noon the next morning, my mother and Astrid Fjeld dressed Ildri in the now-completed bridal gown and positioned her on an elegant Queen Anne low-backed straight chair placed at an artful angle so that the tip of her nose and the curve of her chin could be seen from the street. The chiffon veil, attached to a wide satin band, was set on the crown of Ildri's head and fastened under her coiled hair, which glistened like copper under the streamers of delicate Norwegian lace. The tulle train flowed over the back of the chair to the floor. One hand rested in her lap and from the other dangled a perfect long-stemmed lily, which looked as if it had grown out of the watered-silk folds of the bridal skirt.

When the noon chimes began to strike, Astrid Fjeld instructed my mother to put on her hat and coat and stroll up and down the other side of Nicollet in order to observe how passersby reacted to Ildri's presence in the window.

The first person who came along, a young man in a business suit obviously hurrying out for his lunch, was well past the window before he noticed Ildri out of the corner of his eye. He stopped suddenly and backed up a few steps. He looked cautiously in every direction to see if the coast was clear before he craned his neck to get a better view of Ildri's face. Stepping back to get an overall view, he put his hands in his pockets and shook his head back and forth in open admiration, then hurried on. Three women with shopping bags congregated in front of the window for a long time, pointing and gaggling, and my mother caught the words, "Don't you know watered silk when you see it, Penelope?" When two or more men came along together, they turned their heads but didn't stop. A man walking alone, my mother noted, was snared as surely as if his foot had been caught in a leghold trap.

Astrid Fjeld received two orders for wedding dresses that week. The following weekend the *Minneapolis Tribune* ran a headline over its "Man Around Town" column:

## WHO IS THE BEAUTIFUL WOMAN
## IN THE WEDDING DRESS?

Pedestrians rushing back and forth on their lunch hour this week are being stopped cold in their tracks by a hauntingly lovely woman in a wedding gown, who sits each day at noon in the window of Astrid Fjeld's emporium on Nicollet Avenue. Intriguingly, her back is turned to the street, but passersby are treated to a fleeting glimpse of a sculptured chin, the tip of a pleasingly rounded nose, and the flutter of enchanting burgundy-black eyelashes. Our guess is that the wily Mrs. Fjeld will have more orders for bridal gowns than she can handle. But take care, Madame Fjeld, that you lock your bride up at night along with your gown, for at this very moment I know a dozen ardent would-be bridegrooms with white chargers champing at the bit to carry the fair lady off . . .

In the following days it became obvious that people were coming downtown during the noon hour just to see Ildri. At times as many as a dozen elbowed for position on the sidewalk. Ildri became so nervous she couldn't keep her chin from quivering when she was in the window. She begged Astrid Fjeld, without success, to let her off. Before the second week was out, however, a handsomely dressed man wearing a bowler and a diamond stickpin in his ascot entered the shop and in a heavy Danish accent boldly offered Astrid Fjeld twenty thousand kroner for the wedding gown—provided the woman in the dress went with it. Enraged, the shopkeeper showed him to the door and told Ildri her window-sitting days were over.

The promotion stunt had already served its purpose; Astrid Fjeld now had five more orders for wedding dresses and found it necessary to hire three additional seamstresses. Even after the June bridal season was over, her business continued to increase to such an extent that she rented additional space at the end of the building and enlarged her shop.

❖

Ildri went home for the Christmas holidays, and when she returned she gave Astrid Fjeld notice. Her father had broken off with the woman he had planned to marry; Ildri could no longer withstand his pleas that she move back home. My mother was desolate. She and Ildri had become very close, although they were quite different. My mother loved the way Ildri planned everything in advance, doing her Christmas shopping in June so she could trim her Easter hat in December. On the other hand, Ildri stood in awe of my mother, who could work with such incredible speed and efficiency under pressure that she seldom found it necessary to plan ahead.

When Ildri told Astrid Fjeld she was leaving, she made a surprising request. She asked the shopkeeper whether she might buy the wedding dress she had worn in the window; she would stay long enough, she said, to work out the price of the dress. Astrid Fjeld's chin had dropped and she had cried, "But, Ildri, I didn't know you were getting married!"

"I'm not," Ildri had replied, "but perhaps some day I will. You know how I like to be prepared. It would make me feel so secure to know I had the dress, and I have come to love it so much!"

The dress had not been sold because the prospective brides who came in to look at it found that either the size was wrong or the price tag was too high; the flour baron had expensive tastes. So they had ordered the style in less luxurious fabrics, leaving off whatever frills they couldn't afford.

Astrid Fjeld extracted two months' work out of Ildri in return for the dress, a time my mother thought was much too long, considering that Ildri had been responsible for the dressmaker's increasing prosperity. Ildri herself cheerfully worked out her time, and then she packed the beautiful gown into her mother's antique blue trunk hand-tooled with Viking ships and took it home with her.

◆

Ten years passed before my mother saw Ildri again. Soon after they had parted my mother, too, left Minneapolis to carry out a long-held dream. She boarded a train west and one cold spring day staked out a homestead for herself in northwestern North Dakota, where thousands of acres of virgin prairie rolled two thousand feet above sea level from horizon to horizon. As she lived out the required months of residence in her tiny makeshift cabin, living on potatoes and salt, carrying her water five miles from the nearest creek, barring her door against the coyotes, the big-city world with its Astrid Fjelds and watered-silk wedding dresses seemed as distant as another planet. She came to love the expanse of the prairies so much that wild horses couldn't have dragged her back to the city. She met and married another homesteader, and they built their farmstead from the prairie grass up. The homestead cabin grew to three rooms and a sleeping loft. A windmill, a barn, other outbuildings as needed. The first baby—and then a second and a third. She scrubbed her clothes on a washboard and carried endless buckets of coal to do battle with the harsh North Dakota winters. She helped my father in the fields. Never for a minute did she think that the life she had chosen for herself was not worth it. As the years went by her memories of Ildri became more and more dreamlike. Whenever she thought of Ildri she always pictured her the way she looked in Astrid Fjeld's window wearing the wedding dress.

◈

One midsummer morning my mother was hurrying down a street in Little Butte (my father had driven his family thirty miles into town in their Model T touring car) bent on getting her shopping done so they could get home before dark. She led her blond-headed boy by the hand, and her two little girls were running beside her. Far down the street a woman walked toward her. The lift of the woman's head and the manner in which she walked made my mother's heart come up in her throat. As the woman neared their eyes met. Ildri opened her arms and my mother walked into them.

Ildri was wearing a long high-necked dress of fine blue cotton printed with tiny red-and-white rosebuds. She looked older, my mother said, but was more beautiful than ever. Her once-pale skin had taken on the healthy glow of an outdoors woman, and her auburn hair, now drawn closely to her head, was bright with sunstreaks. In contrast, her eyes seemed darker than ever. My mother had forgotten how striking they were, engulfed in shadow and still tinged with the old sadness.

"Will you look at you," Ildri cried. "Now I know what you have been doing all of these years! Raising a family, and no telling what else." She swooped my mother's small boy up in her arms and hugged him fiercely. "How I wish I had ten of you at home."

"Oh, then you are married," said my mother, "and you got to wear the wedding dress, after all!"

For an instant Ildri's eyes became luminous and her lips quivered—the expression my mother remembered so well —but then she laughed and shrugged. "I wish I could tell you that I did, but that beautiful dress I brought with me to Dakota has never been out of its old blue trunk."

Ildri said that after she had left Astrid Fjeld she had stayed at home and helped her father in the store for five years, and then she had met a young man named Johann Arnstad, who had recently come over from Norway. He had walked into the store one day seeking someone who could teach him to speak enough English so that he could apply for his citizenship papers and be eligible to go out West to homestead. Ildri had taken on the job. They had fallen in love. Johann had gone out to North Dakota with the understanding that if he was successful in staking a claim to a homestead he would send for her and they would be married. Much of the land had already been taken, but he was lucky enough to find a quarter section of land on which another homesteader had relinquished his claim. A carpenter by trade back in Norway, Johann had hurriedly built a twelve by twelve homestead cabin and had then sent for Ildri, who came out by train.

"It was the last of March and ten degrees below zero and two feet of snow on the ground," Ildri said. "I had the wedding dress with me, but I would have frozen to death in it. We went to the courthouse and got married by a judge. Then Johann and I had to drive like the wind by horse and sleigh to reach our claim before dark."

My mother started to cry. *"Kjaere, kjaere,"* Ildri whispered. "Perhaps yet some day I will find a use for the beautiful gown."

Nothing would do for Ildri but that my mother and her family should come for Sunday dinner. When my mother told my father about miraculously running into her old friend, my father said, "She is married to Johann Arnstad? Your friend is Johann's wife?" It turned out that my father knew Johann well and had driven past his place often because it was on the way to the coal mine; when he saw Johann along the road, they stopped and talked. He had, in fact, also met Mrs. Arnstad once. "She is not a bad-looking woman," my father said.

My mother had thrown up her hands in utter frustration. She always cited this incident as a perfect example of what was wrong with Norwegian men. "They know everything that is going on and they keep it all to themselves!"

As they drove across country toward the Arnstad homestead, my father pointed to a white steeple against the horizon. He said it was fifteen miles distant and when they reached it they would be within half a mile of the Arnstad place. As they neared their destination the terrain became more rugged and a low butte could be seen far to the south—a precursor to the Badlands. When they passed the small white church sitting high on a knoll with prairie grass around it, my father said that Johann had built much of the church single-handed in his idle winter months; he and Ildri had donated the land for both the church and the cemetery that lay behind it.

Now they dipped into a long valley and coming out of it saw the automobile trail spinning up ahead like a ribbon to the Arnstad farm, which appeared to lie flat as a picture against the eastern sky. A small prairie-style house and barn were eclipsed by a tall windmill turning briskly in the wind. A dozen black cows grazed on the prairie grass behind the barn; in their midst was a red-and-white pony, who lifted his head and nickered when he saw the car. As the automobile came to a stop in the clearing between the house and barn, Plymouth Rock chickens scurried in every direction. A man was carrying a bucket of water from the windmill. Ildri came running out of the house, and Johann set down his bucket and came to shake hands. A huge man with powerful shoulders and sinewy arms, he had piercing blue eyes and thick yellow hair like a boy's. His rumbling voice seemed to rise from deep within him. He spoke broken English, liberally sprinkled with Norwegian.

Ildri was wearing the same blue dress printed with rosebuds that she had worn in town. "Come in, come in!" she cried, and then added with a small shrug, "It's just a shack."

My mother said she knew before she went in that it

*The Wedding Dress*

wasn't going to be just a shack, but she wasn't prepared for what she saw.

Johann had built two rooms and a sleeping loft onto the side of their homestead cabin to make the usual prairie-style house, but here is where the comparison ended. Everything in Ildri's house matched the print in Ildri's dress. The kitchen and the front room were wallpapered with the same design. The short ruffled cottage curtains at the windows were made of the same blue material. The kitchen and dining-room tables were covered with it. The braided rugs on the floors were blue, with streaks of the blue print woven through them.

"It sounds strange when you try to describe it," my mother said, "but that house was the coziest, prettiest place I ever saw on the prairie. It was like coming into a blue cocoon. Ildri had kerosene lamps in sconces all along the walls, with silver deflectors that picked up that rose-bud pattern and threw it around everywhere."

"I must tell you about this blue print," Ildri said, laughing. "When Johann and I got married four years ago, my father asked me what I wanted for a wedding present. My father is a storekeeper, you know, and I remembered this pattern he sold in his store, which I had always loved. That tiny homestead shack, which is now the porch out there, was so drab I could hardly stand it, so I told him to send me as many rolls of wallpaper and as many bolts of this cotton percale as he could spare. And do you know what he did? I think he did it as a joke and wanted to clear out his storeroom as well. He sent me over a hundred rolls and bolts of this same pattern—not only in blue, but in red, green, yellow, and white. Johann had to take the lumber wagon to bring it home from the freight office. I've got it stored in the hayloft."

Ildri crossed her arms and hugged herself. "But you know how I am. You know how good it makes me feel to know that I have it. It's like money in the bank. When I get tired of blue, I'll cover it with the red. For wallpaper and fabric, I am fixed for life!"

Johann shook his head back and forth and roared with laughter. "This woman . . . this woman!"

My mother said that as long as she knew Johann, these were his favorite words. He never in all of their married life got over the wonder of Ildri.

As they sat down at the dining-room table, which Ildri had set with the blue-and-white Scandinavian china her mother had brought from Norway, Ildri sighed and said, "I'm not much of a cook."

She served up roasting chickens stuffed with apples and nuts, Norwegian meatballs in gravy, mashed potatoes floating in butter, three kinds of homemade bread, and two kinds of wild berry preserves. When she brought in the rhubarb pie, she sighed again and lamented that her hand had slipped so badly on the crust that she was ashamed to bring it out.

"The crust was, of course," my mother said, "perfect. It flaked off our forks."

After dinner Ildri told Johann and my father to take the three children out to the barn for a ride on the red-and-white Indian pony they had seen as they drove in. It was Ildri's pony, a wedding gift from her husband. She had named him Ringebu after her mother's place in Norway.

"I ask this woman what she want for a bride's gift, and she say a pony," said Johann, "so that is what she get. And she ride him sidesaddle up and down these hills."

Alone in the house, Ildri and my mother climbed the stairs to the sleeping loft where, Ildri said, they could have a quiet time to themselves. My mother was surprised that it wasn't wallpapered with the blue print but was instead plastered and painted white. They sat on the large brass bed covered with a gold-and-white quilt stitched in the double-wedding-ring pattern.

"I will wallpaper the walls in the red print when the children start coming," Ildri stated matter-of-factly. "We will move our bed down to the front room, and Johann will build trundle beds for them up here. This loft is roomy enough for as many as want to come."

Throwing open a cedar storage chest at the foot of the bed, she said, "I want to show you my layette."

In addition to a hundred white flannel diapers and dozens of flannel nightgowns embroidered in every conceivable pattern and color, there were tiny morning coats fastened with satin ribbons, flannel baby blankets appliquéd with kittens and puppies, crib quilts stitched in intricate designs, booties with fanciful tassels, and knitted baby bonnets in every color of the spectrum. The last garment that Ildri pulled from the chest was wrapped in tissue paper. She unfolded it carefully and held it high for my mother to see. It was an ivory satin baptismal dress trimmed in exquisite wide lace at the hem and sleeves and stitched across the bodice with seed pearls.

"This all of my children will wear," said Ildri softly. "Both the boys and the girls." She caressed the dress with her hand for a moment before she folded it back into the tissue paper and returned it to the chest along with the other garments.

"Now!" she said firmly, pressing her lips together. "Shall we look at the wedding dress for old times' sake?" She reached under the bed and pulled out the antique blue trunk in which she had packed the dress when she left Astrid Fjeld.

"No!" my mother said, tears streaming down her face. "I don't want to see it."

Ildri pushed the trunk back under the bed. She sat down and put her head on my mother's shoulder. "How I wish I could cry like you. That is my trouble. I cannot cry."

◆

Ildri and my mother saw each other two or three times a year in the following years—always during the Christmas holidays if the roads were open. Ildri and Johann would come to spend the day, bringing gifts for the children: for the girls handmade rag dolls with blue French knots for eyes and for the boy each year a bigger rocking horse named Ringebu. And for all of them crisp *pepparkakor* gingersnaps shaped into snowmen, Christmas trees, steepled churches, and angels. Ildri would hold my mother's children, stroking their hair and remarking that the happiest days of her life would be when she had some of her own.

My mother had her fourth child and then her fifth, and each time Ildri managed to make the trip across the miles to see her before her lying-in period was over, bringing the traditional Scandinavian sweet soup of dried apples and raisins.

Ildri with the years became more and more preoccupied, my mother said, with getting her household tasks done ahead of time. She began to wash her clothes on Friday so they would be ironed by Monday—when all of the other farm wives were hanging theirs on the line. She did her spring housecleaning in January and her fall housecleaning in July. It irritated her that she couldn't plant her garden in March so that she wouldn't have to do it in May.

When she was forty years old, she gave away the layette.

She shrugged it off as of little account.

"My young neighbor down the road from me here was about to lie-in, and she didn't have a stitch to her name for the child except a dozen diapers and a few cotton shirts, and what is that?"

"You gave away the baptismal dress, too?" my mother had blurted out in anguish.

Ildri had looked at her strangely. "Could God have forgiven me," she whispered vehemently, "if I had held *that* out from all the rest?"

◆

It was not long afterward that she let the wedding dress go.

She told my mother about it the day she showed her the new wallpaper.

My mother and her family had stopped at the Arnstad place on the way home from Little Butte to invite Ildri and Johann for Easter dinner. Ildri had told Johann to take my father and the five children out to the barn to see the newborn calf while she took my mother into the house. The entire house was white with red rosebuds. It was so brilliant and sparkling that it took my mother's breath away, but she didn't think it was as cozy as the blue had been. When they climbed the stairs to the loft, my mother noticed that Ildri had grown somewhat heavier and that the fine streaks of gray in her auburn hair were turning it golden. She was surprised to see the new wallpaper in the loft. Ildri remarked that since it now appeared there would be no children she might as well have the loft match the rest of the house.

As they sat on the edge of the bed, Ildri said, "I am glad you are not going to ask to see the wedding dress, because

*The Wedding Dress*

it is not here. My neighbor's girl was getting married to a farmer down the road, and would you know all she had to get married in was a dark skirt and a sweater? A skirt and sweater! Can you imagine? You and I thought times were hard when we were in Minneapolis, but it was nothing like out here in Dakota.

"The more I thought about it, the more I thought, how can I live with myself knowing I have this wedding dress made of the finest silks and satins, yes, even Hardanger lace, mind you, and what is it doing but catching dust under the bed, so I took it over to the girl, and it fitted her perfectly, and you should have seen the stars in her eyes."

My mother was crying. "You understand," Ildri said quickly, "that I didn't *give* it away. She will return it after the wedding and it will be mine again."

❖

Because there had never been a wedding gown remotely like it in the region, the word got around, and it was not long before another bride-to-be showed up at Ildri's door and asked to borrow the dress. In the next few years there was scarcely a summer month when the gown wasn't out on loan. When it became soiled, Ildri would wash the dress in cold water and Ivory soapsuds, always rinsing it in blue-ing water to keep it from yellowing and storing it in a heavily blued muslin sheet.

Occasionally a young woman would come who was too large for the dress, and then Ildri would have to turn her down; when the frugal Astrid Fjeld had cut out the dress, she had left only a minimum seam allowance. Who needed generous seams on a dress that would be worn only once? If the bride was tiny, however, Ildri lightly basted in tucks wherever they were needed and adjusted the hem.

◈

Ildri and my mother celebrated their forty-fourth birthdays together. It was February. A raging North Dakota blizzard had the previous week hurled twenty-eight inches of snow on the ground in twenty-four hours. The prairie lay frozen from horizon to horizon under an unbroken expanse of glistening impacted snow. The children walked on top of it to school, but the country roads were impassable by motor vehicle. My father had spent every waking hour burrowing a path from the house to the barn and other farm buildings. My mother had been housebound for days.

On her birthday she had looked out of the window and had seen like a miracle a Norwegian cutter sleigh pulled by a red-and-white pony skimming on top of the hardcrusted snow. It was Johann and Ildri. Ildri had brought a high angel food cake swirled with her famous burnt sugar frosting and a few candles. They could stay only an hour or two because they had to get home before dark. Ildri had lit the candles while my mother poured the coffee. The four of them had sat around the table as the early afternoon sun bounced off the snow and streamed in through the windows. Johann and my father discussed the weather at one end of the table while my mother and Ildri sat at the other end exchanging confidences. Ildri said that she had had to retire the wedding dress. "When I washed it the last time it was so thin and frail I knew it would never hold in another bride. I think it has earned its rest."

She gave my mother a small white box tied with blue ribbon, saying that it contained the wedding veil. She said it was good as new, because she had never had to wash it. She told my mother to hide it away until her first daughter was married, and after that it could be passed down to all of her other daughters. My mother protested that the veil should have been left with the dress. "No, no," Ildri answered firmly. "Whatever happens I want you to have it. Never again will we see such beautiful Hardanger lace."

Then she had leaned toward my mother and whispered, "Do my eyes deceive me, or is the apron getting snug again?"

Yes, my mother replied, much to her surprise she would be having another child in the spring.

My mother always spoke of this visit with Ildri and Johann as a golden moment in time that happens only once or twice in a lifetime. Everything was so perfect. The unexpectedness of the two old friends appearing from such a distance over the seemingly insurmountable expanses of snow. The quiet of the house with all the children in school. The brilliance of the sun pouring in through the windows. The happy farewells as Johann helped Ildri into the sleigh and tucked the laprobe around her. The tinkling of the sleigh bells as the pony Ringebu gaily carried them across the snow-covered prairie and over the horizon.

◆

Winter came to an end, the snow melted into the creeks and sloughs, the prairie began to green up, and my father started his spring plowing. My mother grew ponderous with the weight of the baby. One midnight she and my father were awakened by a pounding on the door. It was Johann. Ashen faced, he said that Ildri was dying. She had been riding Ringebu sidesaddle over the hills ten days ago, and the pony had stepped in a badger hole and had thrown her. The back of her head struck a rock, knocking her unconscious. The pony had come running to the barn with his reins dragging. Johann had mounted the pony and given him his head, and Ringebu had taken him to where Ildri lay. After stanching Ildri's wound with his handkerchief, Johann had revived her with water from the nearby creek, and then he had lifted her onto Ringebu's back and led the pony home. The wound had at first seemed superficial and had healed over, but brain fever had set in. The doctor, who had finally been persuaded to come out from Little Butte, could do nothing for her. Now she had sent him to bring her dearest friend, whom she must see once more.

My mother hurriedly dressed, and after giving my father instructions for the children, she got in Johann's car. They

*The Wedding Dress*

drove silently across the dark prairie, arriving at the Arnstad place as first light streaked the horizon. One of Ildri's neighbors, holding a kerosene lamp in her hand, opened the door. My mother took the lamp and heavily climbed the stairs to the loft. Ildri was lying under the coverlet, her face flushed and her dark eyes glittering with fever. Her hair was uncoiled and sifted over the pillow like spun gold; it was now the same color of gold, my mother noted, as the cloth that Ildri had stitched into the double-wedding-ring pattern of the coverlet.

Ildri reached out a hand to my mother and then ran it gently across my mother's distended abdomen. "I would not have brought you here if I had known you were so near to lying-in," she whispered. "But, *kjaere,* my friend, you I had to see one more time."

She told my mother to pull up a chair to the bed. She gripped my mother's hand. "The wedding dress. It is in its old trunk under the bed. Is it so willful of me to want to wear it just once?"

She lay back as if to sleep, then suddenly tugged at my mother's hand. "I have shared it all of these years. Is it so wrong to want to take it with me?"

"No, no, of course you must take it," my mother answered.

"Then there is one thing you must do for me. I am no longer thin enough to get into it. Take it home with you, cut it up the back, and sew strips up and down so they can tie me into it. There is no time to lose. Johann will take you home now to your children. He will return for the dress when the time comes."

Trying to find some last words of comfort, my mother said, "You know I can do it, Ildri. You know how fast I can work!"

Ildri suddenly had smiled radiantly. Two hard bright tears appeared at the edges of her eyes and ran down to the pillow. My mother moved to wipe them away, but Ildri stopped her. "No, let them go. I have not felt tears since I can remember."

❖

The children were still in bed when my mother arrived home; they hadn't even known she was gone. All that day she struggled with herself, trying to decide whether to cut into the wedding dress. Despite what the doctor had said, she held out a desperate hope that Ildri would recover. How could she give her back the dress if it were rent down the back? She went to bed that night wracked with grief and indecision but awoke at midnight with the strong premonition that she had waited too long. She lit the kerosene lamps in their sconces on the walls and put the extra leaf in the table. Then in the quiet of the night while her family slept she opened the blue trunk for the first time and lifted out the wedding dress.

"You must remember," my mother said, "that I hadn't seen the dress for almost a quarter of a century. When I touched it I got the strange feeling that it had taken on a life of its own. It was as though an electric shock went through me. The dress was nothing like I remembered it. It didn't look like a wedding dress anymore. It looked like a shroud. All of those blueings had turned it to silver. It was so fragile I scarcely dared touch it. I spread it out on the kitchen table, and when I started to cut it up the back, the watered silk seemed to part itself, with no pressure from my scissors."

My mother whip-stitched the raw edges under, and then, grateful that she had many yards of satin ribbon on hand from which she made her daughters' hair bows, she hand-stitched lengths of ribbon to the edges. She couldn't decide what to do with the tulle train, which she had had to remove. She finally stitched it back to one side. Streaks of daylight appeared through the windows before she was finished. She had just folded the dress and returned it to the trunk when she heard Johann's automobile coming down the road, and knew her friend was dead.

◈

The small white church that stood on the grassy knoll across the valley from the Arnstad homestead was so packed with people at Ildri's funeral, my mother said, that they overflowed onto the steps and into the churchyard as the service began. Inside, the women and children sat on the wooden benches and the men stood at the rear. The last bride to wear the wedding dress, pregnant and weeping, sat in the back row, her blond-headed husband standing behind her. The first bride who wore the dress, now a plump matron with three children, sang "Tenderly Sleeping" in a surprisingly young and sweet soprano. The coffin at the front of the church was open.

"She was all silver and gold," my mother said.

Johann chose to sit alone on his bench in the first row, far to one side. At no time did he look toward the casket. When the service was over, the minister had gone to Johann and, gently taking him by the arm, had asked him if he didn't wish to look at his wife one last time. Johann had got a terrible look on his face and had replied in his resonant voice, which carried all the way to the rear of the church, "Do you not think I already know how she look? Nor will I be the first to forget. Put the lid down." Then he had turned and walked quickly down the aisle and out into the spring sunshine.

That night my mother had to send my father for the midwife, and the next morning I was born. My mother very nearly named me Ildri; but she decided it would be too sad. I was such a happy baby, she said, and finally she gave me her own name. I am proud of it. Still, if she had chosen to name me Ildri, I would be proud of that, too.

When my mother concluded her story, one of us always asked, "What happened to Johann?"

We knew, of course, what happened to Johann, but we wanted to hear it again. Because this is one part of the

*The Wedding Dress*

story that my mother always told in exactly the same way —even using the same words.

"Johann?" she would say. "After a couple of years, like so many homesteaders who lost their wives out here for one reason or another, he went back to the Old Country hoping he could find another wife as good. Well, the woman Johann brought back could speak good Norwegian, all right, but that was about the end of it. She was plain, but no one would have held that against her if she had known how to make bread. After a while the wallpaper started peeling off the walls, and even though the barn loft was full of new rolls she didn't turn a hand to use any of them. She made three trips back to Norway and the third time she didn't come back. I believe Johann thought it was just as well. Now he keeps to himself."

My mother lifted up the palms of her hands. "After all, when you've been married to Ildri . . ."

# 2

# Bank Night

*After months of going to the Thursday night movies* with one goal in mind, Pleasant Anderson wins the $250 cash prize at Bank Night. A trifling amount, you might say, unless you keep in mind that we are talking about 1936 in Little Butte, North Dakota. It hasn't rained—really rained —since 1929. The prairie is brown and hard as a hazelnut. I am ten years old and have never seen an umbrella. Stacked up against the dust storms, the grasshopper blights, the armyworm invasions, and seven-years-in-a-row crop failures, Pleasant's good fortune is a windfall of monumental proportions.

Little wonder, then, that my mother and I are startled

when Pleasant, who is running the combine for my father during the wheat harvest (three bushels to the acre), lurches into our farm kitchen the following morning and heaves a sigh strong enough to waft the red dimity curtains.

"Ya! I done it," he moans reverently. "Won the two hunnert and fifta dollar at Bank Night."

He tosses his Minnesota Paint cap into a corner and leers at my mother, who purses her lips and looks away. My mother has never seen a movie herself, has no desire to see one, and considers anything won at "the show" as ill-gotten gains. Pleasant cranes his neck and tries to peer into the parlor to see whether, by another stroke of luck, he can catch sight of at least one of my four older sisters. No way. My mother has banished them to the sleeping loft. I am the only daughter allowed in the kitchen when Pleasant comes in to meals because I am still straight as a stick.

My mother's caution is well advised. Fifty years old and a bachelor, Pleasant Anderson is generally acknowledged to be foolish about women. No one in the territory has ever actually seen him with a woman, but according to Pleasant himself, he has what he always terms "heavy dates" every Saturday night, and if any woman between the ages of thirteen and forty absentmindedly smiles at him or even says hello, she might very well learn through the grapevine a few days later that she has had a heavy date with Pleasant.

*The Wedding Dress*

This is why my mother keeps her four other daughters under lock and key whenever Pleasant enters the house for meals. She thinks her best hope of keeping their reputations intact is the out-of-sight out-of-mind concept.

My mother motions Pleasant to the table and says, "Now you sit right up, Pless. I got your favorite this morning. Thick sour cream for your bread with rhubarb sauce to go on top."

"Ya, that's good!" Pleasant sighs; in town where he operates and lives in a service station when he isn't hired out, he has crackers and sardines for breakfast. He pulls a red handkerchief from his pocket and mops his flat small-boy face which has a turned-up nose and round diaphanous blue eyes incongruously encased in a man's leathery skin. He gives his thick brown hair a few licks with a stubbed-off comb and swings his tall angular frame over to the table.

I come out from behind my mother because I love to watch Pleasant Anderson eat. First he takes his knife and weaves it in and out of the fingers of his left hand. Then he takes his fork, prongs down, and weaves it in and out of the fingers of his right hand. He is now ready to set to. At no time in the course of the meal does he ever unweave his tools, even to drink his coffee. I have never figured out how Pleasant can drink from a cup without stabbing his eye out, and I want to be around when it happens.

"So then, what are you going to do with all that money,

Pless?" my mother can't resist asking, even as she shakes her head and looks scandalized.

Pleasant cranes his neck and makes another fast reconnaissance of the parlor. He gives a huge sigh of resignation and jams his fork into his bread and sour cream. He eats heartily for a few minutes, and then his eyelashes begin to flutter. "Ya. I got a heavy date tonight," he whispers.

❖

My father, who is waiting for Pleasant out at the rig, offers to give him the day off, but Pleasant says no, he will work his usual hours. Late in the afternoon I am riding with my father on the tractor as it pulls the combine round and round the sparse wheat field (it takes a good half-day to reap a hopperful of grain) when my father suddenly stops the tractor and shouts back at Pleasant.

"Ya! Pless! We're knocking off early today. I know you want to get into town and spend some of that Bank Night money."

Pleasant gives a giant shrug, and instead of loping over to his '29 Chevy and taking off, he reaches for the oil can and deliberately begins to oil up the rig. My father stares in disbelief.

"Ya, Pless. You don't need to oil up tonight. We can do it in the morning."

Pleasant pumps the oil can up and down. "Guess this is one night they'll be waiting for me until I git there," he whispers softly.

Not expecting Pleasant to stick around for supper, my mother is surprised when he takes time to eat a leisurely meal. He has three helpings of fried potatoes and asks for the salt-pork plate twice. Afterward, he even pushes his chair back and leans it against the wall and puts his feet up on the rungs. He spends some time with the toothpick, all the while craning his neck to look into the parlor. It is, as usual, deserted. He sighs, aims his toothpick at the coal bucket with enormous care, and says, "Ya! Guess I'll drive into town."

◆

What happens in Little Butte that night comes to us secondhand; no one in my family ever goes into town at night, the reason being that my father has one ironclad rule for keeping us out of trouble: *Never monkey around after dark.*

But there are at least fifty eyewitnesses to one or another of the events of that night, and in the following years the story is told and retold so frequently that I have almost come to believe I was there. This is the way I remember it.

Although it is early evening, there is still a lot of August daylight left in the North Dakota sky when Pleasant Anderson drives into Little Butte in his black '29 Chevy and parks in front of the Diamond Rail saloon. He slides out from under the wheel and gets out on the passenger side; the door on the driver's side has been stuck for years.

That's a garage mechanic for you, everyone said; he can fix other people's machines but not his own. A mean northwest wind, as it often did in the Dust Bowl years, has blown up at approaching sundown, and the tumbleweeds are rolling through town faster than the traffic. (We had an adage for the wind in those years: *Blow before eleven, still before seven.* When the wind had blown all night and the dust had sifted into the house and between the sheets and down our throats, the belief that the wind would die down before sunup was often the only thing that brought us through the night.)

Pleasant lists into the wind as he heads into the Diamond Rail. After years of standing on farm machinery in heavy winds, Pleasant has a permanent list. I still have a snapshot that someone took of him and me standing on my father's combine in the summer of 1934. He is listing at least twenty degrees off perpendicular.

Launching himself into the saloon, Pleasant stands in the swinging doors for a moment, his legs spread apart. The men at the bar lift their glasses of beer to him, and one of them shouts, "Ya! Pless! Tell us how it feels to be a millionaire."

Pleasant shakes his head and laughs noiselessly. Striding to the bar, he puts a foot on the iron rail and looks around for the barmaid, who is busy at the other end of the counter. For years, ever since the theatre was built back in the twenties, Pleasant has been asking the Little Butte barmaids to go to the movies with him. But the barmaids come and go—not only at the Diamond Rail but at the Silver Dollar across the street and even at the Brass Lantern down at the railroad tracks—and they all treat him the same way. They draw his beer and, wherever he happens to be standing, whiz it to him along the bar so he must catch it. And they all say, "Not tonight, Big Boy."

But tonight—tonight Pleasant figures it will be different.

The barmaid on duty is Big Red—not to be confused with Little Red, who tends bar across the street at the Silver Dollar. Big Red is not tall, but she is a yard wide. Along with a homespun brown dirndl skirt, she is wearing a dark red shirt to match her hair, which frizzes out in all directions. Her arms are muscled up like a stevedore's. Tonight when she sees Pleasant at the other end of the bar she not only doesn't whiz his beer past him, she doesn't even draw it. She walks over and sort of nuzzles up to him over the bar and croons, "Well, Big Boy, I hear you ran into quite a piece of luck!"

Pleasant searches the barmaid's eyes for a moment. He sighs softly and lets his eyes wander up somewhere between the liquor bottles on the high shelf above the counter.

"Whiskey!" he says.

Big Red raises her eyebrows and turns back to the counter and pours him a glass of whiskey and sets it in front of him. Pleasant painstakingly unbuttons the breast pocket of his bib overalls and draws out a thick wad of folded bills. He pulls one off and drops it on the bar. Big Red takes the twenty-dollar bill and rings up fifty cents on the cash register. She puts a ten, a five, and four one-dollar bills in front of him. She presses the remaining fifty-cent piece into the bills and smiles into Pleasant's eyes. He sighs, lets the money ride on the bar, and knocks back the whiskey in one gulp.

"Beer!" he whispers hoarsely.

Shrugging angrily now, Big Red draws a beer, takes the half-dollar off the bills, rings up fifteen cents, and drops a quarter and a dime back on the bills. She places her elbows on the bar in front of Pleasant and cups her head in her hands.

"Say, Big Boy! You know what's playing at the Grand tonight? *Mutiny on the Bounty!* With Clark Gable. I can get off for the first show at 7:30 if I want to. That's only a few minutes from now."

Pleasant lets his eyes wander up to the high shelf again. He takes a great draught of beer and wipes his mouth with the back of his hand.

"I seen it," he says.

A titter runs up and down the bar.

"Las' night," he adds, exhaling heavily. Someone guffaws and the titter becomes louder.

Big Red whirls around and clatters glasses against each other on the counter. The mantel clock on the high shelf strikes the half hour. Galvanized, Pleasant drains his beer and scoops his change from the bar and stuffs it into his breast pocket. He takes off his Minnesota Paint cap with one hand, combs his hair with the other, and says, "How about you and me taking in the show, Red?"

◆

Half of Little Butte seems to be watching Pleasant Anderson and Big Red walk the block down from the Diamond Rail to the Grand Theatre. The wind has picked up and is gusting through town at about forty miles an hour. Automobiles are diagonally parked solid along the street, and people are standing in groups on the sidewalk, their backs against the wind. As Pleasant and Big Red proceed down the street, automobile horns and shrill whistles accompany them every step of the way. Pleasant walks apart from Red and a little to the back, somewhat like a cutting horse bringing in a stray calf.

Someone shouts, "Ride 'em, cowboy!"

At the ticket window, Pleasant says, "Two!" and grins knowingly at the ticket girl as he hands back some of his lucky money.

There are no reports as to how Pleasant and Big Red comport themselves at the movie. After all, people who have paid good, hard-to-come-by money (forty cents for adults, twenty-five cents for students, and fifteen cents for children under twelve) to see Charles Laughton and Clark Gable in *Mutiny on the Bounty* would be silly to take their eyes off the screen. But when the movie is over, about two hours later, a strange thing happens. The crowd standing around the theatre waiting to get in for the second show sees Pleasant and Big Red come out, and at least three people hear Pleasant tell Big Red that he wishes he didn't have to break up their date so soon, but he has to get back to the farm because he has a hard day's work ahead of him in the morning.

Big Red gives him a surprised look, grunts, and says if that's the case she might as well go back to the Diamond Rail and help out until closing time at midnight. So Pleasant again walks down the street with Big Red, a little apart and to the side, and says, "See you tomorrow, Red," as she disappears through the swinging doors of the saloon.

At this point, however, instead of getting into his Chevy and driving out of town, Pleasant jaywalks across the street and heads straight into the Silver Dollar. He again makes a grand entrance, parting the swinging doors and standing against them, his legs spread wide. The men at the bar greet him with mock amazement.

"Ya! Pless! You tired of red hair already?"

Laughing his noiseless laugh, Pleasant strides up to the bar, and the barmaid, Little Red, greets him effusively. At this stage of events, Little Red—who isn't a redhead at all but a rather washed-out, wheat-colored blond—seems to be the only person in the whole of Little Butte who doesn't already know about Pleasant's earlier date with Big Red.

"Well, Big Boy!" she says warmly. "Where have you been? I thought you'd never show up!"

This sends the men at the bar into paroxysms of laughter, and it amuses Pleasant, too. He demands whiskey, again paying for it from the wad in his breast pocket—which isn't lost on Little Red. He orders beer as a chaser, and when the cuckoo clock on the side wall strikes ten, he wipes his mouth with his hand and tips off his Minnesota Paint cap.

"How about you and me taking in what's left of the second show, Red?" he says.

When Pleasant and Little Red walk the block back down Main Street to the Grand Theatre, the summer light has finally faded from the sky and the street lights are on. Now the automobile horns take on the raucousness of a shivaree. Someone shouts, "Ya! Will you look at Clark Gable there!"

Someone else whistles shrilly and calls out, "Hey, Red! When Big Red gets wind of this you better watch out!"

Pleasant shakes his head and laughs, and now he walks beside and close to Little Red with the air of one who has spent the better part of his life escorting women to the movies. When they reach the theatre the wind is trying for hurricane velocity; the metal marquee is swaying and whining overhead as Pleasant buys the tickets. He winks broadly at the ticket girl, and then he and Little Red hurry in to see *Mutiny on the Bounty*—Pleasant for the third time.

In the next hour the crowd on Main Street disperses, and many people get in their cars and go home; but a short while before the movie is over, others arrive and stand around in small groups waiting for friends who are in the theatre. They are surprised to see Big Red charging up the street, her hair frizzing wildly out from her head and her dirndl skirt billowing in the wind. Her eyes are blazing. She storms up to the ticket window.

"Are they in there?" she shouts through the aperture.

"Who?" says the ticket girl, shrinking back.

"Why, that two-timing son-of-a-jackass Pleasant Anderson and that you-know-who from the Silver Dollar. I'll teach him to play up to me one hour and go across the street the next, the damn fool!"

Big Red rushes past the ticket window and into the theatre, trying to sidestep the usher. "Hey, wait a minute! You can't go in there without a ticket," he says, and grabs her arm.

"Don't need no ticket," Red cries. "Just want to fix a couple of guys."

"You do your fixing out on the street, Red," the usher says. He is a husky man, and he also owns the theatre. He twirls Big Red around and swiftly pushes her out past the ticket window and back onto the sidewalk.

"Don't worry, I'll wait!" she says, tossing her head.

Soon Big Red has attracted more people, who stand

with their backs to the wind listening to her threats and waiting to see how she'll fix Pleasant Anderson.

"Why, when I get through with that hunk of farmhand ham," she says, "there won't be enough breath left in that double-crossing body of his to blow out a match."

It is going on toward midnight when the theatre doors open and the people start pouring out. Pleasant and Little Red are among the last. Pleasant is rubbing his eyes. When he sees Big Red, his face flushes deeply. He shakes his head and begins to laugh.

Big Red rushes forward and grabs Little Red by the arm and with a powerful twist sends her hurtling into the crowd. Then Big Red faces Pleasant, who, still laughing, is standing, stunned, with his mouth open.

"Now, Pleasant Anderson, I'll fix you."

She reaches into her handbag and takes out a tiny revolver, the one she has kept under the bar for years, and she levels it at Pleasant's chest.

"Double-crossing two-timer," she says, and fires.

Pleasant is still laughing when he clutches his hand to his heart and falls to the sidewalk. The metal marquee over the theatre is whining so loudly in the wind that no one in the crowd actually hears the shot. But an old woman who lives in a tiny apartment above the First National Bank building at the end of the block says later that she had just opened her door to let her cat out and heard it clear and sharp. She says her cat ran back in and wouldn't go out the rest of the night.

What to do with Big Red after the shooting is no problem. She goes to jail and pleads guilty to a reduced charge of second-degree murder, spends a couple of years in the state penitentiary, gets out on probation, and is soon back at her old job at the Diamond Rail and attracting customers from as far away as Montana and Canada who want to hear how she fixed Pleasant Anderson.

What to do with Pleasant himself is not so easy. He has no family, no religion, no burial plot, and nobody wants to claim him. He has always been tight-mouthed about his youth, saying only that an uncle, who homesteaded in a distant part of North Dakota, brought him over from Norway and didn't want anything to do with him after that. The part that doesn't ring true, of course, is Pleasant's name; everyone knows he couldn't have been given *that* one in Norway.

When none of the Little Butte churches show any inclination to give Pleasant a Christian burial, my father persuades our country church, the Prairie Norwegian Lutheran, to take him—although Pleasant has never actually lived in our community. Our church, too, is somewhat of a closed corporation, because the only persons buried in the cemetery are the homesteaders—just a few of whom have already passed on—and several of their babies who died of scarlet fever. But there is, after all, plenty of room: a five-acre spread behind the church with little more than a dozen graves rattling around in it.

It takes my father and the neighbors most of one day to dig Pleasant's grave; it isn't easy to dig a hole six feet deep in ground that hasn't been rained on for seven years. Little Red, who feels a certain amount of guilt for what happened, contributes a blue serge suit that belonged to her late father. Luckily, this fits Pleasant to a T, and everyone who comes to view him at the funeral home remarks how nice he looks in his bronze coffin, paid for by his Bank Night winnings—of which he had spent only $2.90.

In planning the church service, my father and the organist argue with the pastor over the choice of hymns. The pastor, determined to make an *example* out of Pleasant, wants the congregation to sing "Though Your Sins Be as Scarlet." The organist, who is a farmer six days a week, sides with my father that this is hitting a man who can't rise up to defend himself, and he says he can't play an unfamiliar hymn with four flats on such short notice. "There Is a Green Hill Far Away" is substituted. They all agree that the service should end with "Bringing in the Sheaves," because Pleasant, having worked on so many of the old threshing rigs in the early days, has brought in as many sheaves as any man in his time.

The day of the funeral is uncommonly quiet; the wind, for once, is still. In the cavernous church—optimistically built for a much larger congregation—the men sit on one side of the aisle and the women and children on the other.

I sit to my mother's right, and to her left, lined up beside her on the wooden bench, are her four older daughters, dressed, at her request, in their white Confirmation dresses. My mother turns her head and her eyes sweep along the row of daughters—a dazzling blur of white—and a proud smile flits across her face. I think she is trying to make it up to Pleasant Anderson for all of those times she locked her daughters in the loft when he came in to meals. It might occur to her, too, that today their reputations are not in jeopardy.

Thwarted on his choice of hymns, the pastor makes it up in the sermon. He speaks of the wages of sin and the dire consequences (pointing down from the pulpit to the coffin) of frequenting saloons and movie houses and getting into the wrong kind of company. In conclusion, he strikes his fist and intones, "All they that take up the sword shall perish by the sword!"

The women bring out their handkerchiefs and sniffle and weep, but on the other side of the aisle the men sit with their arms crossed against their chests and look straight ahead.

After the service my father and the organist and four of the other neighbors carry the coffin out to the grave, which is set quite a distance from the other graves; with all that room, there is no use crowding. Beyond the cemetery, the North Dakota prairie, baking brown in the sun, stretches from horizon to horizon. The men lower the coffin, and after the pastor has thrown down the first clod of dirt and has pronounced his "Dust thou art to dust returneth," he and the women return to the church, leaving the pallbearers and the rest of the men to close the grave.

The men take off their suit coats and hang them on some headstones. The other children and I stand around to watch them as they take up their shovels. At first the thuds are loud and metallic, but as the grave fills up they become more and more muted. The men alternately stop for a moment in the blazing sun to take out their handkerchiefs and wipe the perspiration from their faces.

One of the men breaks the silence.

"Old Pless didn't have no sword, that's for sure."

"He didn't have no gun, either." *Thud, thud.*

"Big Red was the one had the gun."

There are grunts of assent all around. The men heap up the dirt into a smooth round on the grave and tamp it firmly down. They retrieve their suit coats from the headstones and throw their shovels over their shoulders. As they walk back toward the church, my father beckons to me and takes my hand.

One of the men squints at the brilliant sky and says, "Could be clouding up to rain."

My father looks quickly up at the sky. "You joshing, Carl?" he says, and we go to the automobiles, where the women are waiting.

# 3

# The Skaters

*If I am ever going to tell Borghild's story, it had best* be now. It is true that one becomes more farsighted with age—but only up to a point; my distance vision, I sense, has reached its outermost limits. One thing is certain: the bonds between Borghild and me were strong. We grew up together—second cousins, best friends, both daughters of homesteaders. Borghild chooses to stay and I leave, but I am only as far away as the Empire Builder. Scarcely a summer passes that I don't board that noon train out of Chicago. I can still hear the conductor's voice rasping out the stops: LaCrosse, Winona ("Wine-oney!"), St. Paul, Minneapolis, Willmar, Breckenridge, Moorhead, Fargo, Devils

Lake, Rugby, Minot, Stanley. I have now ridden half a day and all night, it is gray dawn, and I can look out of the window and see for the first time the familiar bare brown rolling hills. My throat tightens up. I get my luggage together and draw on my gloves, knowing that in an hour the next stop will be Little Butte. I envision my aged parents standing expectantly along the tracks. The year comes when they are not there. But I still have the cousins —even they are diminishing in number—and the bare hills and the lone butte.

◈

Borghild once told me that if she had used her good sense she would have got rid of the snow globe that Ingval had given her. At least hidden it in the back of the cupboard instead of letting it sit on the kitchen table where Gunnar could stare at it. It was a small globe—scarcely bigger than the sugar bowl—and inside it, the snow granules whirled around three skaters: a scarlet-clad girl with yellow pigtails and two boys in blue wearing Norwegian visor caps.

It was the summer the rains came back to the plains that her brother-in-law had given her the globe. He and Gunnar, who together farmed the homestead that they had inherited from their immigrant parents, were in a jubilant mood as they watched their wheat fields greening up after eleven barren years in the Dust Bowl. The two of them walked around the farm whistling and springing up on the balls of their feet as if there were coils under them.

Ingval had come home from town one day and, when he walked into the kitchen, had gaily tossed the globe at her.

"Catch, Borghild! Christmas in July!"

Coming in from the barn later, Gunnar spotted the globe as he sat down for coffee at the kitchen table.

"What in thunder is this thing?" He picked up the globe and turned it in his hands, making the snow granules whirl around the skaters taking long strides on a tiny round pond.

"Ingval just brought it to me from town," Borghild answered as she poured his coffee.

"Why, that son of a gun!" Her husband shook his head and laughed.

From then on, the globe seemed to hold a strange fascination for Gunnar. He seldom sat down to the table without turning it over and staring through the whirling snow at the skaters.

When they were sitting down to supper one evening he said, "If one of those boys fell down and broke a leg, would the other two just keep skating?"

"Those three are not even skating in the first place," Ingval said. "They are locked into their stride. It's the white granules that make them look like they're moving."

"Don't you think I know that?" said Gunnar hotly.

"What I want to know," Borghild interjected, "is whether those two boys will keep skating if the girl falls down."

Another day as they were sitting at breakfast waiting for

her to serve the wheat cakes, Gunnar shook the snow globe and wondered, "Where do these people come from, anyway? They're Norwegians, you can tell that by the caps on those boys. Do they live on a farm or are they city folks?"

"The only place they are from is the factory where somebody made them," said Ingval.

"That girl doesn't look like anyone I ever knew," Borghild said quickly, putting the wheat cakes and a pitcher of boiling syrup on the table.

"Oh, I don't know." Gunnar turned and glanced pointedly at his wife. "She puts me a little in mind of *you*, Borghild, in your younger days. Wouldn't you say so, Ingval?"

Looking down at his plate, Ingval answered in a low voice, "I've always marked it."

Surprised, Gunnar looked sharply at his brother and reached for the syrup.

❖

Borghild told me that she could remember nothing in her life before she was in love with Gunnar. Her earliest memory was as a three-year-old sitting on Gunnar's lap and playing with the brass buckles on his overall suspenders as he bounced her up and down on his knees. Even at fifteen, he had this great booming laughter that almost blew her off his lap. Even then, she loved the smell of him. He smelled like warm cow's milk, sweet-clover hay, Palmolive

*The Wedding Dress*

soap, and oily hair tonic. She remembered being five and sitting on Gunnar's lap at the table while they ate cream porridge out of the same bowl and his younger brother sat across laughing at them. When at age seven she walked down the road to country school, Gunnar and Ingval often drove past in their black truck and stopped to give her a ride. She sat between them along with the grease cans and wrenches, and when they reached the white frame schoolhouse which had prairie grass growing up to the door, Ingval would swoop her off the seat, throw her over him, and deposit her at the side of the road.

When she was twelve, she began spending much of the summer at the Ivarson farm, running errands for Gunnar and Ingval's mother, who had been widowed when the boys were small. The Ivarson farm adjoined her parents' farm. The houses were a mile apart if she took the road, but if she cut across the cow pasture it was only half a mile. Mrs. Ivarson thought the sun would not rise and set if her sons weren't brought their midmorning and midafternoon coffee wherever they were working on the farm, and it was Borghild's job to bring it to them. If the boys were working together—cutting hay or shocking wheat—they always insisted that she sit down and share their food. They pressed frycakes and sandwiches on her and warned her that she would never grow up to be anything but skinny if she didn't start eating.

The two boys didn't look as if they came from the same family. Gunnar was stocky and ruddy, with thick rye-colored hair and penetrating cornflower-blue eyes. Ingval was slender and dark-haired, with lazy brown eyes that could suddenly light up and dance. He was so tall that whenever he went through the doorway of their low-slung farmhouse he had to duck his head to clear the lintel. If he wasn't doing farmwork, he either had his head in a book or he was sketching or painting pictures in his loft bedroom. Gunnar, on the other hand, was all business. The farm was his life.

When Gunnar was working alone cultivating corn, he would let Borghild ride with him for a few rounds. He would point out a pheasant running along a fencerow or a crow that lurked overhead ready to swoop down and caw at them. Sometimes they even saw an eagle flying so high in the brilliant North Dakota sky it looked as if it were on another planet. If the bobolinks were singing, Gunnar himself often broke into song. His favorites were "The Old Rugged Cross" and "Battle Hymn of the Republic." He would cut down the motor, and his beautiful baritone would rise above the sound of the tractor and, it seemed to Borghild, float up into the heavens to blend with God's voice itself.

She hated Saturday nights because Mrs. Ivarson would send her home before dark—just as Gunnar and Ingval had taken out their strops and razors and were getting ready to go to a dance. She stood by and watched jealously during the next few years as Gunnar cut a wide swathe with the township girls his age—and she breathed sighs of relief as they all married other men. I once asked her if she didn't think it strange that Ingval didn't have a lot of girlfriends, as good-looking as he was. "Ingval? Good-looking?" She looked at me, surprised.

❖

When Borghild was eighteen, Gunnar came home one day and found her sitting on Ingval's lap.

It had happened so innocently. Mrs. Ivarson had been kneading bread dough in her capacious bread pan, which she always placed on a kitchen chair because she was too short to reach the metal mixing board that pulled out of her cabinet. (Her six-foot husband had made it for himself, she always pointed out, when he was still a bachelor.) Borghild was standing beside her, sifting flour into the pan. Ingval was sitting at the table drinking coffee and eating a bowl of cream porridge left over from breakfast. Mrs. Ivarson never threw away food. It was always recycled sometime during the day. Ingval suddenly remarked, laughing, "Remember, Borghild, how you used to sit on Gunnar's lap eating porridge from his bowl?"

Mrs. Ivarson, who loved a good joke, shrieked, "Now, Borghild, you show Ingval how you are still not too old to help him finish off that cold porridge!"

Taking up the dare, Borghild herself shrieked and dropped down in Ingval's lap and wrested his spoon from him. They all were red with laughter when Gunnar opened the door and walked in.

He stopped short and flushed hotly as his eyes took in the scene. "What in thunder goes on here?"

Taken aback at her son's wrath, at the same time amused at what her mischief had wrought, Mrs. Ivarson clamped her mouth shut. She blinked rapidly several times and began vigorously kneading her dough. Borghild stiffened and froze on Ingval's lap.

"I think we have had enough of this foolishment," Gunnar said. He pulled Borghild up. "Could a man find a cup of coffee around here somewhere?"

His mother lifted her hands out of the dough and scurried to the stove to push the coffeepot forward.

◆

After that, everything was different. Gunnar had instantly decided that Borghild was *his* girl, and he was not in the habit of making lukewarm decisions. He courted her fervidly and one June evening married her in the country church as the last bright rays of the sun hanging low in the west streamed through the open windows.

For their wedding dance afterward at the town hall, Gunnar had hired a trio of violinists to play Norwegian folk dances. She and Gunnar danced the first dance alone. He then took an obligatory turn with his mother and all of the township ladies, young and old, who were sitting against the wall. Borghild, in the short blue-silk wedding dress her mother had made for her, danced until she was ready to drop with every man in the township between sixteen and eighty—with everyone, that is, except Ingval, who didn't show up at her side until almost midnight, and then his face was flushed and he had an exaggerated offhand manner.

"Where have you been?" she asked impatiently. "I've been waiting for you to ask me to dance for hours." She scrutinized him closely. "From the way it looks, you haven't been standing back in the corner with our mothers all night eating *kransekake* and drinking coffee."

"Oh, you know these wedding dances," Ingval answered airily, his eyes glittering. "The refreshment outside of the hall is always stronger than what's inside." He swooped her out on the dance floor as the fiddlers started a spirited *springer* dance.

You had to hand it to the Ivarson boys, she thought resignedly, even in their cups they could outdance any man on the floor.

"Surely, sister-in-law," said Ingval with mock Old World formality as they danced, "you cannot deny me a kiss on your wedding day." He bent his head and brushed his lips chastely across her cheek.

Gunnar took her on a short honeymoon to the Black Hills, and then he and Ingval brought her things over from her parents' farm. It wasn't as if she were moving anywhere, because she had been at the Ivarsons' much of the time anyway. In fact, she got along better with Mrs. Ivarson than she did with her own mother, who was forever cleaning and washing walls and curtains and dusting the undersides of the dresser drawers, which Borghild thought was going too far. Mrs. Ivarson thought that having good food and a good time was more important than always to be seeking out dirt, and this is the way Borghild felt to a T. They also had an identical way of shrieking when they were happy or angry.

At first Ingval insisted that he was going to move out, but Gunnar thundered and raised such a fuss that he finally consented to stay. "Our father left this farm for both of us," Gunnar said. "It's your home as well as mine." They built an extra room on to the house for their mother, but she had only a few months to enjoy it. She dropped dead one day when she was hanging clothes on the line.

◆

Gunnar and Ingval were good to Borghild—as good as they had been to their mother, which was very good, indeed. They always saw to it that she had a fresh pail of water from the well and a bucket of coal for the stove before they went out, and never did they return from town without bringing her something special—a bolt of calico, a small sack of peppermints hidden at the bottom of the grocery bag, a shiny new thimble, or a bright pair of mittens.

Times became harder and harder as the Dust Bowl years began to pile one on another. Her husband and brother-in-law saw their fields repeatedly shriveled by drought and wind, then ravaged by hordes of grasshoppers swooping down in a cloud so great that it blotted out the sun. The time came when Gunnar and Ingval were forced to plow up their blackened fields in order to feed the Russian thistle roots to their livestock. The next year there were no Russian thistles. One dreadful weekend in August the brothers, their faces drawn and gray as ghosts, participated in the government-ordered county roundup of ten thousand starving cattle—several dozen of them their own—who were herded across country to the Little Butte stockyards. The weakest animals were killed, and the stronger ones were shipped to fresh Georgian pastures. The government paid fifteen dollars a head.

In those terrible barren years of the thirties, Borghild was barren, too, and she despaired that she and Gunnar would ever have a child. But when the rains began to come back to the prairie at the end of the decade and even the cottonwood trees which had been dormant for years began to leaf out, Borghild felt, like a miracle, new life stirring in her. Gunnar was beside himself with joy, and for the first time in years she heard him out in his fields singing again, in his great booming voice that rolled up to the heavens, "Mine eyes have seen the glory of the coming of the Lord . . ."

The day the baby was born, Ingval brought her a china doll that said Mama when its stomach was squeezed. Gunnar roared with laughter and bellowed, "If you didn't know better, you'd think Ingval was the father!"

The brothers had only a year or two to enjoy good crops

and a new beginning of financial security before the war broke out after Pearl Harbor. The draft board routinely left one able-bodied man on every farm and conscripted the others. Gunnar had a wife and baby, so he was the logical one to stay, and Ingval was drafted. The day Ingval went to town for his army physical, Gunnar was inconsolable, pacing his fencerows hour after hour and refusing to eat. "They should have taken me instead," he moaned. "Ingval doesn't have the temperament for the army. He's too easy-going. They'll run over him like a harrow. He's never been away from home before."

"You haven't, either," Borghild pointed out.

"I'm tough, though. I've got a hide like a buffalo."

When Ingval finally drove in at sundown, Gunnar rushed from the barn to meet him as he got out of the pickup. "Well, boy, how did it go?"

Ingval was dark-faced. He plunged his hands deep into his pockets. "Didn't want me. Those yahoo doctors said my ticker was too noisy."

◆

After that, as winter came on, Ingval spent more and more time up in his loft bedroom, painting. He had started doing pencil sketches when he was a child. As he grew older, his mother had bought him an easel and brushes, and he had moved on to watercolors and oils. His paintings of the farm and its seasons now covered almost every wall of the house. Although he had never before painted a portrait, he asked Gunnar a few weeks before Christmas if he could paint Borghild as a Christmas gift for him. Gunnar said sure, go ahead, he thought that would be fine. She wouldn't need to sit for him, Ingval said, laughing, he already knew what she looked like.

As Christmas neared, Borghild became wildly curious to see how Ingval was coming with her portrait, but every time she went up to the loft to clean his room, he had his easel covered and securely tied with string. On Christmas Eve after the baby had been put to bed, Gunnar brought in the tree, as he customarily did, and set it up in the corner of the kitchen. Ingval and Borghild trimmed the tree while Gunnar strung red garlands crisscross from each corner of the kitchen and hung a great red paper bell from the center where the garlands crossed. They were in a festive mood by the time they finished. Gunnar brought out a bottle of Aquavit and the wineglasses his mother had brought with her from Norway, which he chilled for a minute in the snow outside the kitchen door. They held their glasses high and toasted each other with the fiery spirit.

Ingval said he couldn't think of a better time to unveil the portrait. As they started to climb the stairs to the loft, the red paper bell fell to the floor, taking all of Gunnar's garlands with it. He told Borghild and Ingval to go ahead, he'd be up in a minute. The two of them continued up to the loft, and Ingval lifted the cloth off the easel and stood back to let her examine the portrait.

She stared at it, and then her face, already flushed from the Aquavit, grew hot as fire.

"You don't like it," Ingval said.

"It . . . doesn't look like me!"

She couldn't bring herself to say that he had made her too beautiful.

It was as if she had suddenly looked into her mirror and had seen herself as she had always wanted to look but knew she never would. Ingval had softened her square face into the suggestion of an oval, had made her gray eyes enormously large and wide apart, and had painted brilliant lights into her flaxen hair. He had dressed her in Norwegian costume. She was wearing an ivory-colored linen shirt with a high ruffled neck and over it a red brocaded vest. There was something vaguely familiar about the portrait, as if she had seen it before.

*Gunnar will see that it doesn't look like me,* she thought desperately, and pressed her hands to her face. As though reading her thoughts, Ingval became suddenly defiant and called down the stairs.

"Come on up here, Gunnar. It seems your wife is not happy with the portrait."

Gunnar came bounding up the stairs. He looked back and forth from Ingval, standing with his arms crossed, to Borghild, wringing her hands. Then he looked at the portrait. He studied it carefully from every angle, turned to his wife and examined her face, and then went back to the painting. Finally he made his judgment.

*The Wedding Dress*

"A better likeness I have never seen! I cannot understand you, Borghild. Ingval has done a *bee-utiful* job. This good I did not know he could paint." He pounded his brother on the back. "Now what I want for it is a good frame. Next time you drive into town pick one out and I'll pay for it. I'll hang it over our bed. It's the only wall space left in the house."

His arms still crossed, Ingval lounged against the wall. He glanced at Borghild, and suddenly his eyes danced.

At that moment she remembered who the painting reminded her of. It was the girl in the snow globe—grown up.

❖

It seemed to Borghild that the years in which her daughter grew up were the briefest in her life. She had no more than turned around, she always said, before her daughter had married and left home and it was the way it had always been—just her and Gunnar and Ingval. And the older she became, the more she forgot her childhood on the adjoining farm. Unless she thought to remind herself of it, she found herself thinking that she, too, had been born in the house in which she had spent all of her married life. When she walked across the cow pasture to her parents' old farm, where someone else now lived, it was as if the girl who had lived there was a childhood friend who had grown up and moved away.

The three of them were not young anymore.

The snow globe had yellowed with age, and now it looked as if the skaters were gliding around in a dust storm. It depressed her because it reminded her of the Dust Bowl years, which she would rather forget. Sometimes when she cleaned off the kitchen table she would consider storing the globe away, but she always decided that its absence would arouse more questions rather than less, so she ended up letting it remain on the kitchen table between the salt-and-pepper shakers and the sugar bowl. Besides, Gunnar hadn't mentioned the snow globe for so long that she was certain he was finally seeing through it without thinking about it.

It was the day after he had been to the doctor, who had told him that it was about time he started letting up on some of his farm work, that Gunnar referred to it again. Ingval, whose tall form was now so stooped that he didn't have to duck his head anymore to clear the lintel, had just gone out the door to start the morning chores, and Gunnar had lingered over his coffee. He suddenly picked up the snow globe and twirled it and twirled it in his hands.

"What happens when one of these boys dies?"

◆

It was not long afterward when he came home one day and told her that he had bought a house in town. It was a very small old bungalow but it was full of furniture, he said, and he had got it all for a good price from Old Man Jensen and his wife who were moving into a rest home. There wasn't a thing wrong with that house, Gunnar said, that a new roof and some paint wouldn't cure.

In one of the rare times that she had blown up at her husband, she shrieked, "Now why in the world would you do a thing like that? Now I have two old houses to clean and fix up instead of one!"

Trying to quiet her, Gunnar said in a low voice, "You know good and well, Borghild, that when I die you cannot keep living here with Ingval. It would not look right and people would talk."

She stared at him and blurted out, "But we are so old now!"

Her husband stared back at her unmovingly and shook his head.

❖

Gunnar said that he and Ingval could put on the new roof and paint the house themselves, because they were good with their hands and had always done their own carpentry. He asked her what color she wanted the house.

"Suit yourself," she shrugged. "It's your house."

In September after harvest was over and they had their autumn plowing done, the brothers spent every day in town tearing off the old roof and pounding on new shingles. Every time she drove into town with their coffee and saw the two old men tottering unsteadily about on the roof she grew weak in the knees and shrieked up at them, "Now you two watch yourselves. As old as you are, neither one of you has got any business running around up there like schoolboys!"

One day she drove up and saw them on ladders painting the house. They were painting it pink. She began to cry. They pretended not to see her. She set their coffee on the driveway, turned the car around, and went home.

They worked until long after sundown the day they finished painting. She had been pushing their supper around on the stove for two hours when they finally dragged into the kitchen, gray with fatigue. She had made their favorite dish, black pudding fried in butter, but they were too tired to eat; they sat drinking cup after cup of coffee.

Rising stiffly from the table, Gunnar said, "Do not get up, Ingval. I'll do the milking. You did most of the work today."

Sitting quietly for a few minutes after Gunnar had gone out, Ingval was lost in thought and absentmindedly stirred his coffee. And now, strangely, it was he who picked up the snow globe and twirled it in his hands.

"There is no reason now, Borghild," he said in a low, urgent voice, "why you and Gunnar cannot move into town one of these days soon, before the cold weather sets in. I have always wanted to bach it out here, but you never gave me a chance."

"Don't worry, you won't be seeing *me* moving into that

*The Wedding Dress*

house until—" she burst out fiercely, her words dropping in midair as she realized that Gunnar hadn't told his brother the real reason for buying the house.

"Sure you will," said Ingval soothingly, and then he unexpectedly smiled at her so tenderly that she grew confused and looked away. "You two wouldn't want to be out here by yourselves once I go, anyway."

"Where in the world are *you* going?" she cried out in alarm.

"I am getting old, Borghild. Nobody lives forever."

"But you are younger than Gunnar!"

"A man's age cannot always be counted in years."

She went white. She got up from the table and walked around to where he sat. She stood behind his chair for a moment, then bent down and brushed her lips across his cheek.

"Do you remember, brother-in-law," she said, her voice shaking, "how you kissed me the night we danced at my wedding?"

◆

Now that the house in town was finished and ready for occupancy, Gunnar seemed to become a different person. While always before it was Ingval who had started the "foolishment," as Gunnar called it, it was now he himself who found small things to joke about. He never went to town without bringing her home something silly: a jack-in-the-box, a tiny yellow windmill to stick in the front yard and whirl in the breeze, or a potato peeler with ten gadgets attached. One day he brought her a Ouija board, which Borghild refused to touch because she thought it was witchcraft; so he talked Ingval into trying it with him, and they sat with their gray heads bowed over it all one evening, laughing boisterously as they let it take them where it would. It was a long time since Borghild had seen them so light-headed.

They stayed up so late that, for the first time in years, Gunnar beat his brother, who was an early riser, to the breakfast table. She had already dished up the cream porridge and poured the coffee when Gunnar sat down alone. Borghild sat, too, and took a sip of coffee.

"Ingval must have overslept," she said.

"Do not worry about Ingval. He has never missed breakfast yet."

Gunnar poured milk on his porridge and began to eat. She went to the stove and picked up the coffeepot, then set it down again.

"Ingval's coffee is getting cold," she murmured fretfully to herself.

Gunnar looked at her sharply. He pushed back his chair and slowly climbed the stairs to the loft.

She sat down at the table and twisted her fingers over the steam from her coffee cup. The cuckoo clock struck seven times. No sound came from the loft. The coffeepot gurgled and hissed on the stove and then was quiet.

Waiting, she abstractedly picked up the snow globe and rolled it back and forth between the palms of her hands.

"Borghild! Come on up here!"

Gunnar's shocked voice rolled like a thunderclap down the stairway. She jumped, and the globe dropped from her hands to the table and fell on its side. When she set it upright she saw that the skaters had broken loose from the pond and were floating around freely in the snow granules.

She gave a thin wail, ran to the stairway, and saw Gunnar waiting, ghost-faced, on the top landing.

"It was supposed to be me," he said.

"No, no," she replied as she hurried up the stairs, her arms outstretched to comfort him. "It was all of us."

# 4

# The Nights of Ragna Rundhaug

*When we saw this* ancient *lady come driving up our* lane in her well-preserved black Essex Coach, which she called her "machine," we shouted to our mother to hurry out of the house to greet her, and then we stood back and laughed nervously. We knew that the old woman would alight from the high automobile wearing her black crepe dress and the black pearls falling to her waist, and she would have on her black Enna Jettick shoes with her ankles swollen over them. The skin of her face and neck would be all run together like that of a plucked boiling hen, and she would shake our hands and say we were her children and call all of us by the wrong names. My mother would invite her in, and the queer lady would pull up a kitchen chair to the cooking stove and when the heat got to her face her birdlike eyes would go vacant and she would "turn off," as my mother called it.

Taking us into a corner, my mother would admonish us in whispered tones to have some *respect*. Hadn't she told us dozens of times that Ragna had delivered close to a thousand babies in her time? She would remind us that there was never a week back then—and not so far back, either, considering how young some of us were—that Ragna hadn't been driven across the countryside (often in a snowstorm and always at night, the way my mother told it) by a frantic homesteader whose wife was walking the floor back home, staving off the labor pains by sheer willpower until her husband returned with the midwife. My mother would point to each of us and say, "She delivered you and you and you, and most of your friends and hundreds of others who are grown up with children of their own." Our awe renewed, we would back away from Ragna and let her stare in peace into the hot stove.

◆

*She hadn't started out to be a midwife. Far from it . . . had been dragged into it, protesting all the way. Why couldn't they have left a maiden lady alone who wanted nothing more than to sit in her homestead cabin with her white dog and her chickens out back and her horse in the shed ready to be hitched up to the*

*buggy anytime she took a notion to go to town? But no*
*. . . never could she have got out from under it unless*
*she had given up her homestead and her hard-won*
*independence and moved back to Wisconsin, and*
*never would she have done that.*

◈

It was Junius Johnson's fault, she would have to say that.
Old Junius was the one who had started it. If it hadn't
been for him, she might have been left in peace to her
crocheting. But no, the drunken fool had to come around
and play on her soft nature, and more than once, too. She
would like to have forgotten those times, *wished* she
could forget them, but they were etched on her memory
as if a branding iron had put them there.

It must have been two or three o'clock in the morning
that first time old Junius came banging on her door. It had
scared her spitless. Country folk didn't come pounding on
your door in the night unless there was a prairie fire; this
was March with a fresh foot of snow on the ground and
still snowing. Vittehund had set up a terrible barking—
clawing and throwing himself at the door. It was all she
could do to fling a wrapper on and get to the door before
he splintered it. When she opened it, there was Junius—
he was a young man then—in his coonskin coat and cap,
covered with snow from head to foot, rasping and heaving,
his breath curling out of him in wisps like from a rusty
teakettle.

Behind him in the darkness she had seen his box sled and his team of dapple-gray plow horses snorting and stamping as they tossed their heads to clear their nostrils of the falling snow.

"Oh, it's you, Junius," she had said.

"The wife. In a bad way," he gasped.

"Jennie?"

"Went into labor last night. I went to get Mrs. Inge, but she's over in the next county delivering a baby. I just do not know where to turn, Ragna Rundhaug," he had whined in that high thin voice, which never failed to surprise her coming out of such a huge swarthy man. "I thought maybe you could come and see what you could do."

"You better come in, Junius, so we can shut this door. No, never mind the overshoes. My floor is used to snow."

Junius had stepped over the threshold, and she closed the door after him as he stood panting and wiping the snow from his face. She had pulled her wrapper around her and pressed her lips tightly together.

"Surely you must know, Junius, that I am a spinster. I have no children nor have I ever witnessed a birth. I wouldn't know that first thing to do. Might do more harm than good, as far as that goes."

Junius had stared helplessly at her and passed a wet leather gauntlet over his eyes. "It's just that I cannot stand to see her this way. Just cannot seem to handle it. Just having another woman around would be company for her."

"What about your closest neighbor over there? Mrs. Sundquist has five children of her own and knows about those things. Couldn't she come over?"

"Two of 'em down with the scarlet fever. More'n she can handle now."

"What about Geena Larson, north of you?"

Junius's voice broke. "Mailman brought a telegram that Geena's mother died. She took the train to Minnesota last night."

What could she do? She had got dressed and bundled up against the weather. She had put Vittehund on a chain, and she and the dog had got in the box sled with Junius. He had driven wildly across country through the snow-storm, shouting at the horses and every now and then pulling a flask of whiskey out of the pocket of his coonskin coat to fortify himself. When she had finally rebuked him sharply, saying that there was time enough to celebrate after the baby came, he had complained that he would go crazy if he didn't have something to steady his nerves. By the time they reached the Johnson homestead he was pretty well besotted.

◆

She had tried to forget the dreadful night and day that followed. Had tried to blot out the terror and the guilt. The terror she could deal with. It came at you straight and strong, and you fought it back until you had it licked, and then it crawled away for a while and didn't return until you were strong enough to handle it again. But the guilt was different. It hung on your shoulders like an itch and nagged and nagged, and you were never rid of it. She told it—this hoary creature—a thousand times to get off her back. Why should she feel guilty for being ignorant? For not having the special knowledge to deal with a circumstance that was thrust on her through no fault of her own?

Anyway, she had lost Jennie and the baby. No, *she* had not lost them, that was wrong, wrong. Junius had lost them because they were his. Jennie had lost herself and the baby because it was *her* life she had chosen for herself and she, Ragna Rundhaug, had nothing to do with it . . . at least would have had nothing to do with it if she hadn't been pulled out of her own house on a stormy night.

But the clawing never stopped, and in the following weeks and months her brain never stopped, either. It kept chewing and chewing her ordeal over again like Vittehund worried an old soup bone—like the way he never got rid of it and it kept getting tougher and stringier.

❖

Why she bought the books she could never fully explain to herself—or rather, admit to herself. One day while reading the newspaper that she received every week in the mail from her old hometown in Wisconsin, she had seen a set of medical books advertised. The widow of the old country doctor back there was selling everything off. Old Dr. Veiss. He had brought her into the world. On an impulse she put money in an envelope and mailed it to his widow. When she had gone to the freight office to pick up the box, she had pressed her lips tightly together and didn't say a word when the curious depot agent asked her what was in the box.

For days she had let the box sit unopened under the kitchen table while she sat in her rocker and crocheted. Until one day—when the beast began gnawing at her—she dragged the box out into the middle of the floor and took her bread knife and cut the string and lifted out one of the musty red books. She burned her kerosene lamp to the bottom of the wick that night; the next night she replenished the kerosene in the lamp and kept on reading. All of that winter she read. On the day of the month when a neighboring homesteader came with her load of coal and she knew she would have to ask him in for a sandwich and a cup of coffee, she piled the books back in the box and pushed it under her bed.

It was not that she was going to use this knowledge. Far from it. But at least it would keep her brain occupied so it might stop chewing on the same part of the bone and get a new purchase on something.

The reading was tough going. Even though she had taught school for a few years back in Wisconsin before coming west to homestead, had even gone to normal school and got a teacher's certificate, still all of these medical terms were strange to her, and she had to keep looking up words in her dictionary. When she had finally got through the doctor's books, she thought to herself, "I think if I read them again I would understand a few things," so she started over and read them again.

◈

It was the next winter—the winter after the war in Europe started and some of the neighbor boys were fighting in France (doughboys, they were called, she never knew why)—that the flu epidemic hit so hard. That was the winter people started knocking on her door again. Not to deliver babies. God knew she would never do that again, no matter what (and who would want her after what had happened). But to help out with sickness in the families . . . the high fevers of 104 degrees and more, the terrible coughing. How could she refuse since she was well and had no responsibilities? She and Vittehund had gone from farm to farm that winter, staying a week here and a week there until the families got back on their feet.

One thing she never let on to was that she had read the books. That she ever *owned* the books. Yes, it was true she had learned a thing or two. But if those she ministered to got well, or did not get well, she did not want them to say it was because she had read the books.

When spring drew near that year and the flu seemed to be burning itself out, she had begun to hope that would be the end of it for her, too, and that she could get back into her own little house without interruptions and would again be able to sit in her rocker in front of the stove, warming her feet on Vittehund's back and picking up on her crocheting. She was actually *lonesome* for those crochet needles . . . but, no, if she had known *how far she was from the end of it* she might even then have sold out and gone back to Wisconsin.

◆

It happened over again so much like the first time that if she had told anyone about it they would not have believed her. It was one of the last afternoons in March, when most of the snow had thawed and run into the ditches and sloughs and she had thought there was no way spring was not coming, that it began to snow again. It snowed and snowed, and when dusk came on it was still snowing. The snow was halfway up to her knees by the time she went out to the shed to feed her horse and lock up her chickens. When she looked out across the prairie, the snow was like a sheet of white coming at her and closing in on her. Instead of being frightened at her isolation, she had a feeling of relief. *I am safe tonight. Nobody will come for me tonight.*

She had gone back to her house and lit the lamp and cooked herself a bowl of oatmeal for supper and had given half of it to Vittehund. Then she had put some fresh lumps of coal in the stove and had drawn up her rocker close, and she and the dog had sat there soaking up the heat, snug and warm against the snow piling up on the window.

Vittehund heard it first, leaping up and howling at the ceiling. She had thought—until the pounding came on the door—that there must have been a pack of coyotes outside. When she opened the door, there was old Junius in his coonskin coat, heaving and rasping, as if time had dropped back to that dreadful night. She looked beyond him, and there again were his dapple-gray plow horses, impatiently snorting and blowing and shaking their harnesses.

For one terrible moment she and Junius had looked into each other's eyes.

Junius started to speak, choked and coughed violently, then turned and spat into the falling snow.

Clearing his throat, he turned and faced her again. "I can see that the last person you wanted to come knocking on your door on a night like this is me," he blurted.

"You had better come in, Junius, so I can at least get this door shut," she had answered. And then she had asked—not knowing how cruel the question was until he winced and closed his eyes—"What is it this time?"

"It's the wife," he whispered.

"Your new wife is down with the flu?" she had asked woodenly, knowing better.

"No, no—" Junius's high voice rose and broke. "She's going to have a baby . . . is trying to have it right now."

Her knees had gone weak, and she had had to go to the

kitchen table and grip the sides of it to get a hold on herself.

"Why aren't you over getting Mrs. Inge? She is the midwife!"

Junius sank into her rocker and put his head down. "I was over there. Mrs. Inge is down bad with the flu. She's been taking care of the sick, Ragna, just like you, but it was one too many for her, and she finally came down with it herself. Spreading like fire through her lungs, her old man says."

"Your other neighbors close to you there?"

"All down with the flu. Just when folks thought it was letting up, it's started again."

She had gripped the table so hard she could feel her nails gouging into the wood. "How . . . how can you ask me to do this, Junius Johnson, when you know what happened last time?"

Junius had lifted his head and looked at her, his eyes stripped naked.

"There isn't anyone else," he said.

◆

She had gone with him, of course. There are a few times in your life when there are no choices at all. No matter how much you promise yourself that you *will* have a choice, a time comes when the promises you made yourself aren't worth spit and you do what you have to do or quit living . . .

But this time, at least, she had laid down *conditions.*
She would not come, she told Junius, unless he stayed
sober. And unless he stayed in the house to help her instead of going out to the barn on the pretext of seeing to
the animals, then not coming back for hours and leaving
her alone to cope.

Junius had stood up in front of her, the snow melting off
him in a puddle on her floor, and had sworn to God he
would be a reformed man. With a big show he had taken
his flask out of the pocket of his coonskin coat and handed
it to her—but not before he took a quick strengthening
gulp of whiskey.

She packed her bag and got Vittehund on his chain. As
she was about to latch the door behind her she remembered something. She went back into the house and got
her jar of sourdough starter from her warming oven,
wrapped it in newspaper, and put it in her satchel. One
thing she had learned that winter: whatever happened, it
was comforting to be able to fix some warm food on short
notice.

When they got out to the box sled, a nasty wind had
picked up and the snow was coming down in stinging
flakes, as though it was finally going to settle down to
some real business. For a while the horses followed their
old tracks, but soon these were filled in with fresh snow.
Junius began pulling the reins this way and that, confusing
the horses and swearing and coughing and spitting into
the hard wind. The spittle was blowing right back into her

face as she sat beside him on the springseat, Vittehund at her feet.

It seemed to her that they were going in circles, but she tactfully remained silent.

"You don't think I know where we are, do you?" Junius had suddenly shouted defensively. "I can tell you one thing, Ragna Rundhaug, I know this prairie like I know the back of my hand. We're headed due west. Yessiree, we are headed due west, just like we are supposed to be headed." His voice ended in a high squeak that was caught up and carried away by the wind. He coughed and spit and whipped the backs of the horses with the ends of the reins.

What seemed like hours later, when she was numb with cold and Vittehund was shivering under her feet, Junius pulled the horses to a halt. His black eyebrows and eyelashes were white with snow, and he looked like an old, old man.

"We're lost," he sobbed.

"Give the horses their heads, Junius," she had pleaded. "They'll find their way home."

"These dumb animals? Don't you think I'm smarter than they are? I've heard that story before—folks letting their horses find the way home in a storm. That's a bunch of baloney. Let 'em do that and they'll have us over in the next county before you know it."

"All right, then, Junius," she had answered with a craftiness born of desperation. "If you are so smart, you can just turn these horses around and take me home. I came out here with you for your wife's sake, not to be driven around in circles in a blizzard all night."

Junius sank down beside her on the seat and looked balefully at her for a moment. He tried to brush the snow off his lips. "I could use a drink."

"If I let you have a drink, will you let the horses have their heads?"

He had sneered a little and nodded almost imperceptibly. She reached into her satchel and came up with the flask. After taking a great gulp he handed it back to her, then loosened the reins and wound them around the top board of the box sled. He folded his arms deliberately across his chest and shouted, "Go on! Giddyup!"

The horses started up and after a few yards, feeling no pressure on their mouths, they slowly made a right-angle turn. "See?" Junius rasped accusingly. "Now they're headed *north!* What do they know?"

"Let them go, Junius."

It was not long afterward that the horses came to a dead stop. "See?" Junius shouted into the wind. "Now they're lost, too, worse'n I ever was!"

Ragna had squinted desperately into the night, and she had caught a glint of red at her side of the sled. She leaned far over the side, reached out, and touched wood.

"Isn't this your barn, Junius?"

*The Wedding Dress*

It was all he could do, for his bragging, to find their way from the barn to the house, which was small and low and shrouded with snow. Junius had to kick and beat away the drifts that had piled up in front of the door before they could enter.

A kerosene lamp with the wick turned down low sat on the kitchen table. It was cold in the house. The new wife was pacing back and forth in front of the stove, clasping her hands under her great distended abdomen as if she already had the baby in her arms. She said she had been afraid to venture out to the coal shed to fill the coal buckets. Ragna had never seen Junius's new wife and was relieved to see how tall and big-boned she was. Jennie had been so tiny. The new wife had such a strange name— Ragna would think of it in a minute. She was deathly pale —and who wouldn't be—but she had clear gray eyes with a sensible look in them. She was wearing a white flannel nightgown with her coat thrown over her shoulders. She had uncoiled her hair, which fell in a great flaxen braid to her waist.

Junius looked sharply at his wife and winced. "How goes it?" he asked thinly, and hurried on before she could answer. "Here is Ragna Rundhaug. We just barely made it home in this storm, I can tell you that. Those stupid horses fought me all the way, trying to get us lost, but I managed to get them home!"

Ragna had stared at him, openmouthed. She had never before known a man who was jealous of his horses. Junius grabbed up the empty coal buckets and went back out into the storm with them.

The new wife—Kjersten, that was her name—released one hand from under her abdomen and held it out. "Pleased to meet you," she said. "You better get those wet things off. Junius will stir up the fire and it will be warmer."

Ragna had sat down on a kitchen chair and taken off Vittehund's chain. The dog shook himself and walked over to a corner of the kitchen, where three small children were sleeping on a shakedown bed. Ragna hadn't noticed them when she came in. When she saw them a sharp pain cut across her chest. *Jennie's three boys she had left behind.* Ragna had not even wanted to *think* about these children, had managed to put them back in the farthest recesses of her mind so they did not even exist for her, so that when the guilty spells came these children would not be piled up on the remorse she already had to bear for losing Jennie and the baby.

She went to the bed and looked down at the tow-headed boys sound asleep under a weight of heavy quilts. Vittehund had dropped down beside them. He loved children, thought he was one of them.

*"Stakkars litten!"* she whispered. "Poor little ones."

Ragna turned to face Kjersten. Surely Junius must have told her what happened before; but knowing Junius, maybe not.

Before Ragna could speak, however, Kjersten had

looked directly into her eyes and said evenly, "I'm beholden to you for coming. You must understand that, whatever happens, I will not hold it against you—either for now—or for what happened . . . last time."

◆

She had put Kjersten to bed in the next room. It was the only other room in the house, except for the loft. The boys usually slept up there, Kjersten said, but it had got so cold when Junius was gone that she had had to move them down into the kitchen. She said her pains had started early in the afternoon, and she had sent Junius over to get Mrs. Inge. When he came home at dusk and said the midwife was ill and couldn't come, nor could any of the other neighbors, she had pleaded with him to stay home, not to leave her again, but he had insisted on going back out into the storm to seek more help. She said her labor pains didn't seem to be getting anywhere, that they were no better or worse than they were when they started, and they were just wearing her down.

A thin streak of foreboding had gone through Ragna, but she told Kjersten it was likely that her muscles had tightened up on her because of worry. She fixed her a cup of water with sugar in it from the teakettle that was still warm on the stove and said it would relax her.

Junius came back in with the buckets of coal and had to pull the door with both hands to get it closed against the wind. He put coal in the stove and stirred up the embers, and the fire flamed up. He hawked and spit into the stove and stomped his feet.

"I know I promised you out there in the sled that I wouldn't leave you alone in the house with her this time," he whined, "but if I don't get out to the barn and get them horses under shelter and grained, they'll be stiffer'n dead coyotes by morning, and there goes my spring plowing."

She had told him to take a lantern and go ahead and be quick about it. She took her sourdough starter from her satchel and put it on the warming shelf over the stove. She shook the snow from her coat and hat and hung them on a peg. She listened to the wind howling outside and watched the snow swirling up to cover the windows and wrung her hands. She opened the cover of the gold watch that hung on a chain around her neck. It was five minutes after midnight. Her mother always said that sick people got either better or worse after midnight. Her medical books had no opinion on that. Besides, Junius's new wife wasn't sick. She was just having a baby. *Just!* That was a fine thing for her, Ragna, to think, after what had happened in this house before. She bit her lips, wrung her hands some more, glanced over at the sleeping children, and went back into the bedroom.

Kjersten was sitting up in bed rocking back and forth. It was dark in the room. The kerosene lamp, turned down low, sat on one end of a chest of drawers in the far corner of the room. On the other end was a pile of freshly washed and ironed baby clothes. Ragna turned up the wick and looked for somewhere to sit, but there was no other furniture in the room. She brought in a kitchen chair and pulled it close to the bed. She saw that beads of perspiration had broken out on Kjersten's upper lip.

"My pains just keep coming and coming, but I feel like the baby has got nowhere to come through," she said, trying to laugh. "I suppose every woman feels that way if it's her first time."

"You must push down hard with your stomach muscles so you can make the passage large enough for the baby," Ragna had told her. "That will also make your bag of waters break, and the baby will come on faster."

Kjersten had tried again and again to push and would let out a small scream, cover her mouth, and whisper, "I don't want to wake the boys."

Ragna had finally held Kjersten's hands and then her shoulders, and the time came when they were drenched with each other's sweat.

"It feels as though the baby wants to come in the wrong place," Kjersten whispered again and again.

A despair such as she had never felt had descended on Ragna. She went out to the kitchen and paced the floor and wrung her hands and raged. Could it happen twice in a row—that the same thing could be wrong with the new wife that had been wrong with Jennie? And where was that fool of a Junius? She snapped open her watch. It was well past two o'clock. Had he gotten himself lost coming from the barn to the house? Him and his bragging about how he knew the prairie like the back of his hand. He was likely out in his own barnyard, walking in circles in the snowstorm, telling himself he was going west when he was going south.

She went back into the bedroom. Kjersten was sitting on the side of the bed. Her eyes had lost their sensible look and were glazing over. "Where is Junius?" she cried.

"He went out to put away the horses," Ragna replied in a matter-of-fact tone. "I suppose that takes time. Maybe he is milking the cows."

"No," Kjersten said. "He milked them before he went to get you."

"Well, do not worry about it. I am sure he will be in any minute. I am not a midwife, but maybe if I look at your stomach I can feel what position the baby is in."

When she had put her hands on Kjersten's abdomen, the baby had suddenly given a strong kick toward the mid-section. *That meant the head must be somewhere in the right direction.* She was pulling the bedcover back up when she heard the door slam in the kitchen. She went out to see Junius standing in the middle of the room covered with new snow, a pail of milk in his hand.

"Where have you been?" she whispered, so engulfed with rage that only the children sleeping in the corner kept her from screaming at him and beating him with her fists.

"Well, now, Ragna, I had to milk them cows," Junius

said. "The cows were just bawling to be milked, and I could not leave them 'til morning."

"You're lying," she hissed at him. "Your wife said you milked them before you came for me. How many cows have you got anyway?"

"Six," Junius answered, blinking his eyes rapidly. "That's a lot of cows to milk, and it takes time."

She had looked down into his bucket. "Just half a bucket of milk for six cows? They must all be dry!"

Junius had dropped down on a chair and started sobbing. "You know I cannot stand to see her this way. I stayed out there because I just cannot stand it, Ragna, that is all."

She had pulled up another chair to his and spoke to him in a low voice. "Now you must get a hold on yourself. You have lost one wife and you do not want to lose another. I am not a midwife, but from what I know now I think that what was wrong with Jennie is what they call a breech birth. The baby could not come because it was turned in the wrong direction. If the head does not come first, the limbs cannot make it through the birth canal. I believe with Jennie it was turned so wrong that nothing or no one could have helped her. I may be wrong about Kjersten, but the baby's head seems to be in the right direction. The shoulders might be turned a little so the head does not come right. Another thing, her bag of waters has not broken."

"What can be done?" Junius was trembling so fiercely on the chair that the floor creaked and moved.

"If you will help me, I can try to snip the bag of waters with my embroidery scissors. That will make her labor come fast and hard, and then I can try to push the baby a little from the outside so the head will move better into position."

Junius had broken out into a cold sweat. "I couldn't stand to see it. I just could not stand it, Ragna!"

Ragna had glanced over to the corner of the room to make certain the children were still sleeping.

"There is no other way, Junius. Somebody has to hold the lamp."

She went to her satchel and took out the flask of whiskey she had taken away from him. She took a glass from the cupboard and poured a couple of inches of whiskey into it.

"Here. Drink this and maybe it will steady your nerves so you can hold the lamp without dropping it."

Junius threw back his head and drained the glass. He sat motionless for a minute, gave a final tremble, relaxed, and sighed. "All right. Let's get it over with."

Ragna took the glass and poured some more whiskey into it. She poured warm water from the teakettle into the glass.

"Is that for you?" Junius asked, astonished.

"No," she replied. "It is for your wife."

They went into the bedroom, and Ragna closed the door behind them.

◈

An hour before dawn, when the baby came out, it was so still she knew she had failed again. In the worst kind of despair, she turned the child over and smacked it a good one on the bottom.

The baby screamed in protest.

She had heard the first cries of nearly a thousand babies since that night, but never a cry like this one. Never would she live so long that she would forget it . . .

◈

So then, she had tied the umbilical cord neatly with crochet thread, had wrapped the baby in a blanket, and laid it in the crook of its mother's arm. She told Kjersten that she was going into the kitchen to make her a cup of strong coffee and some sourdough pancakes. Junius was sitting at the table having another drink of whiskey. She had suggested it. There was not that much left in the flask anyway. He had ended up doing fine in there; he had not dropped the lamp.

She peered out of an unfrozen spot in the window and saw first light streaking across the horizon. The snow had stopped, and the wind had died down. The three boys were sitting up on their shakedown bed, wide-eyed that a white dog was nosing them.

"Vittehund! Vittehund!" they exclaimed.

"That white dog is not the only thing that came last night, boys!" Junius shouted expansively.

He went into the bedroom and came out with the baby and brought her to his sons' bed. They stared in wonder.

"Now all you got to do is think of a name for her. Think you can do that?"

The boys giggled, turned their backs, whispered together, giggled, and whispered some more.

"Come on, come on," Junius urged. "You got a name or not?"

The smaller ones poked the oldest to speak. He hesitated, then turned shyly away.

"Speak up!"

"Jennie," the boy said.

Ragna was beating pancakes. Her spoon stopped. She looked at Junius. He had turned to stone. Fearful that he was going to drop the baby, she hurried over and took her from him. An awful quiet had descended on the house. She didn't know how it would have come out if a sensible voice hadn't called from the bedroom.

"As good a name as any, I would say."

Just then Vittehund set up a howl, and a minute later they heard sled runners squeaking on the snow and the jangling of harnesses. Junius roused himself and went to the door. There stood a stranger in a heavy farm jacket and a cap with the leather flaps pulled low over his ears. He had a couple of days of beard on him and was haggard and wet. Ragna looked beyond him out to the barnyard; just enough light was coming out of the east to see his box sled and his team of plow horses, snorting and stamping as they waited. She knew then that it would never end.

"Is the midwife here?" the man asked.

"You mean Mrs. Inge?" replied Junius.

"Mrs. Inge died of the flu last night," the man said, taking off his cap. He looked past Junius at Ragna holding the baby.

"Will you come?"

She had pressed her lips tightly together. "I am not a midwife," she answered firmly. "But I will come. Just this once."

# 5

# The Sins of the Fathers

*Whenever the Vigg sisters, who were secretly alluded* to as the "Wicked Sisters" after the notorious incident involving the Mulhallen boys, drove past the abandoned homestead shack (the scene of the crime) on their way to Little Butte to shop for their respective families, they always looked at each other, raised their eyebrows, and shrugged. As the years passed and they became matronly, they even started to laugh.

"Somehow it doesn't seem to hurt so much anymore," Doreen would say.

Rosella would agree. "Time heals. And to be honest with each other, would we have had it any other way?"

The incident—which was actually more than an incident inasmuch as it determined the rest of their lives—occurred in 1941, that exultant year in which the Dust Bowl and poverty officially ended for many of the Great Plains farmers. The year in which they had their first bumper crop after a decade of drought. The kind of a year they refused to believe could end at Pearl Harbor.

Doreen and Rosella were seventeen and sixteen, the only children of Martin Vigg, whose wife had died in childbirth when Rosella was born. At that time Martin's spinster sister Olga had come west from Fargo to help with the children, but she, too, had died after a few years, leaving Martin to be both father and mother to his daughters, along with the terrible responsibility to bring them up right—to guard their virtue until the day he could marry them off to good and honest men.

The reason this awful burden weighed so heavily on Martin Vigg was that he himself had got their mother into trouble when she was only sixteen. Their parents had arranged a hasty marriage, and although he had loved Marie with all his heart and would have married her in any case, he would regret the rest of his life the shame he had caused her. He had made a solemn promise to himself that his own daughters would never suffer the same fate.

Bastian Mulhallen and his family of six husky boys lived on a farm in the next township ten miles south the way the crow flies. Bastian and Martin had known each other since boyhood, both having grown up on their fathers' homesteads, which they later inherited. They had mutual yet unspoken sympathy for each other because Bastian, too, had been forced into a quick marriage. His wife, Beret, never got over the awful fact that the birth of her first son was forever recorded in the county courthouse six months after her marriage. A bitter woman who kept her family in seclusion at home, Beret had five more sons in relentless succession. When her oldest sons were teenagers, she died one winter of the dreaded "double-lung" pneumonia. The neighbor women who attended her reported that her last words, spoken with a great sigh of relief, were, "Now is the struggle over."

The neighbors had initially felt sorry for Bastian Mulhallen and his motherless boys. The women brought them scalloped-potato casseroles and shimmering bowls of Glorified Rice. It soon became apparent that neither their sympathy nor their food was needed. Whereas before the family had been virtual hermits in Beret's shame, shortly after the funeral Bastian and his boys appeared for the first time ever in church, the boys barbered and scrubbed, the big ones proudly shepherding the little ones. It was as if the family had experienced a renascence with the mother's death. The old house, once steeped in gloom, now had its window shades rolled to the top. The older boys cheerfully cooked and cleaned, washed and ironed as if they were born to it. Neighbors dropping in would often find the older boys baking cookies as the younger ones sat around the table eating them as they came from the oven.

After Bastian brought home a piano, of all things, having talked the piano salesman into giving his sons a few free lessons, all the Mulhallen boys were soon playing by ear. Anyone driving down the road past the place could hear the banging. The neighbors became convinced that the emancipation of the Mulhallens would be ongoing.

◆

One Saturday evening in the late summer of 1941, two of the Mulhallen boys came driving up the lane of the Vigg farm in a glistening new blue V-8 sedan. They jumped out of the automobile and strode boldly toward the house, ignoring the hound who was barking horrendously at them from a distance. The boys were freshly shaved and wearing identical blue serge suits, white shirts, and red neckties. They had broad ruddy faces, startling blue eyes, and straight yellow hair bleached almost white from the sun.

Martin Vigg came from the house and silenced the dog with a word. He shook hands with the boys.

"Mulhallens you are, that I know, but which two of the six I would not want to place a bet on!"

"We're the top of the line," the taller one said. "I'm Floyd and this here is Alvin, and Pa sends his greetings to his boyhood friend."

"Those I will take and glad of it," Martin Vigg answered heartily. "And what brings you boys out of your township today?"

"The last dance of the summer at Bickler's Barn," Floyd answered. "The last is always the best, you know. Of course, Charlie Bickler is always around to run things proper. Alvin here and me were wondering if your girls could go along with us?"

Martin Vigg's heart constricted. *So it has come to this.* These were the first boys who had ever driven to the farm wanting to take his girls somewhere.

Stalling for time to think, he said, "Well, now, Bickler's Barn. That's a mighty far piece. Halfway to the Badlands, and country all the way."

"Yes, sir!" Alvin spoke up, flashing a set of strong white teeth. He pointed to the glistening V-8 that still smelled of fresh paint. "And we got the car can cover the miles. She's primed, revved up, and ready to go. Pa just bought her after that rattling good harvest we had."

Martin Vigg's mind was racing. If it had to be boys, he couldn't think of anybody better than the Mulhallens. They didn't come any finer than old Bastian. On the other hand, he'd heard a few wild stories about the older Mulhallen boys. They'd got into a fistfight at a pool hall in Little Butte a while back. He wished now he'd got the straight of it.

"How about it, Martin?" Floyd asked challengingly,

opening his double-breasted jacket and putting his hands on his hips.

"I guess I'll just leave it up to the girls," Martin said. "You boys wait right here and I'll go in and ask them."

◆

Thirty minutes later the Vigg sisters were in the backseat of the V-8 and the Mulhallen boys were riding up front, speeding southwest across country as the low-hanging sun started to fall behind the buttes in the distance. The seating arrangement was Martin Vigg's idea. When he had escorted his daughters out to the car, he had quickly pulled open one of the doors to the backseat and said, "Hop in, girls. You two ride in back. It's safer back there."

When their father had come in and asked them if they wanted to go, without even bothering to answer they had rushed into their bedroom to change into fresh white blouses and dirndl skirts, along with white socks and saddle shoes. They had thought this day would never come. Their constant lament was that they never got to *go* anywhere. They never got to have any *fun*. During the school year they attended a bleak little high school in town that was just a few rooms tacked on to the consolidated grade school. In the summer they helped their father on the farm. The Vigg sisters could drive anything on wheels—tractor, truck, or combine. Every morning they tossed a coin to determine who had to stay indoors to cook and clean, and every night they wound up their hair on metal curlers in anticipation of a more exciting day to come.

Their radio, a big one with a huge loudspeaker, which their father had given them for Christmas one year, was what kept them going. At night in their room, the radio turned down low, they memorized the popular songs, listened to the big dance bands, and learned to dance by dancing with each other. Their favorite program was Sammy Kaye's "Sunday Serenade." *Swing and sway with Sammy Kaye.* They loved to dance. They were dark and pretty like their mother and looked like twins, except that Rosella had a slight list in one of her eyes, which made her even prettier, and Doreen wore a bossy expression, which people said ruined her looks.

The Vigg sisters knew the Mulhallen boys, but not well. The only place they met was in the Lutheran church, which straddled township lines, but inasmuch as the women sat on the Gospel side of the aisle and the men on the Epistle side, there wasn't much opportunity for eye contact there.

◈

The Mulhallen boys didn't seem to mind the strange seating arrangement at all; they were both too busy driving the car. Floyd was steering and Alvin was calling the turns. They had the front windows rolled down, which was moving their hair somewhat, but nothing compared to the turbulence in the backseat. The Vigg sisters' curls were being lifted off their heads, and they were frantically hanging on to what was left of the hairdos that had been so painstakingly set on curlers the night before.

"How you girls doing back there?" Alvin yelled into the wind, bracing his feet on the floorboards as Floyd braked and screeched around another curve.

"We could use a little less wind back here," Rosella answered in a sweet voice.

"A whole lot less!" Doreen called out bluntly.

Without looking back, the Mulhallen boys rolled up their windows a couple of inches and continued their relentless pursuit of the road ahead.

"This is going to be the last wingding of the year," Floyd shouted. "Gonna have both square dancing and round dancing. That barn loft is so big you could lose a team of Clydesdales in there and not find them until the middle of next week!"

"You girls like to dance?" Alvin shouted, leaning into another curve.

"We hope we'll die on our feet dancing," Doreen shouted back.

"Same here," Floyd said, flinging his head in the direction of the backseat for a moment. "It's going to be quite a night."

Darkness had fallen by the time they reached Bickler's Barn, the longest barn the Vigg sisters had ever seen. Two giant cupolas shone silvery in the starlight. A fat man in a carpenter's apron was standing at the entrance taking ad-

missions. "Mulhallens!" he boomed. "See you got yourselves a pair of *pretty* ones tonight. That'll be a dollar per
couple." The Mulhallens dug in their pockets and came up
with the change. The fat man stamped the back of their
hands with purple ink. Then they followed the stream of
people climbing the rough wooden steps to the hayloft,
which was dimly lit with hanging lanterns on either side.

At one end of the loft, a very old man with an eight-
string Hardanger violin was playing softly and sweetly for
the square dancers while another old man called the sets.
At the other end of the loft, three young men with crew
cuts were playing dance tunes on a piano, accordion, and
guitar.

"You want square or round, girls?" Floyd asked.

The Vigg sisters looked at each other. "We'll take
round," Doreen said. "Square's so square."

"Our way of thinking exactly," Alvin said. "Isn't that
right, Floyd?"

Floyd didn't bother to answer. He put his hand behind
Doreen's elbow and firmly propelled her out on the dance
floor. Alvin followed with Rosella.

The crew cuts were playing "Chattanooga Choo-Choo."
They played "Elmer's Tune," "Green Eyes," "I Got a Gal in
Kalamazoo," and "You Made Me Love You." Someone re-
quested "Waltzing Matilda." Whatever the rhythm, the
Mulhallen boys danced the two-step. Two steps to one
side and then two steps to the other. Whenever Doreen
caught Rosella's eye, she dropped an eyelid. Rosella

dropped one back. After a few rounds, they changed partners, Floyd dancing with Rosella and Alvin with Doreen;
but as the night wore on, they stopped changing partners.
Floyd kept dancing with Rosella and Alvin with Doreen. At
intermission the Mulhallen boys left the Vigg sisters at the
side of the dance floor to go and fetch bottles of Coca-
Cola.

"Isn't this *fun?*" Rosella whispered. "We're finally having
some *fun!* Do you think we'll ever have this much fun
again?"

"Maybe if we stick with the Mulhallen boys," Doreen
whispered back. "I can take Alvin, but Floyd is such a
know-it-all."

"That's okay," Rosella said. "I'll take Floyd off your
hands anytime. Where do you suppose they learned that
two-step? Different, but fun."

"The piano salesman must have taught them," Doreen
said.

At half-past midnight, the crew cuts played "Good
Night, Irene." The old man with the Hardanger fiddle had
tired out an hour earlier and gone home, taking the unwill-
ing square dancers with him. The Mulhallen boys and the
Vigg sisters danced cheek to cheek and then followed the
other couples down the dusty stairway and out to the automobiles.

This time Rosella sat up with Floyd and Alvin was in the
backseat with Doreen.

"How long will it take us to get home?" Doreen asked. "Pa will be worried."

"Don't worry," Alvin said. "This baby will get us home from zero to nothing flat." He was leaning forward between Floyd and Rosella to peer at the road as the automobile picked up speed.

"This is a lonely road at night." Rosella shivered as she looked out at the buttes silhouetted against the horizon.

"Nothing to be afraid of," Floyd assured her. "Nothing out here but raw country."

The road had begun to stretch out into flatter, more familiar territory when the car pulled alarmingly to the right and went *thump, thump.* Floyd braked slowly and managed to bring it to a stop. Alvin leaped out and moaned, "I can't believe a flat on this new buggy!"

Floyd came around from the other side. He combed his hair with his hands. "We got a brand new spare. We can put it on in a few minutes." He looked around. They were stalled across from the abandoned homestead shack they passed every time they went to Little Butte. "Hey, Alvin, let's pull onto the approach to this shack and get off the road. You girls get out to take the load off."

The Mulhallen boys moved the car into the turnoff and put the parking lights on. They opened the trunk, took out the spare tire and two flashlights, and jacked up the wheel. They soon had the spare on and the nuts tightened. They wound the jack down and let the tire down on the ground.

"Dear Jesus," Alvin cried. "This'n's flat, too!"

"It's a new tire and they likely didn't pump it up at the factory," Floyd said. "Just get the tire pump out of the trunk and we'll be on our way in a few minutes."

Standing several feet away, the Vigg sisters looked at each other and raised their eyebrows.

Alvin rummaged in the trunk. "Hey, Floyd, my eyes must be going bad," he said. "I can't seem to come up with that pump."

"Oh, for crying out loud," Floyd shouted. "It's there. You know it is." He pushed his brother away and started rummaging himself.

Alvin walked up to the girls. "Sure it's there," he said. "Floyd will find it."

They heard the shuffling of tools from one side to the other and then silence. Then the lid of the trunk being slammed down. Floyd came around from behind the car. "Darned if I can find the cussed thing, either. They must have forgot to put it in at the factory."

Rosella began to sniff. Doreen put her arm protectively around her sister.

"Look here, boys," she said, trying to keep her voice steady. "This isn't some kind of a bad joke you're trying to play on us, is it? We've heard of this car-stalling-trick-in-the-middle-of-the-night before, you know."

The Mulhallen boys jammed their fists into their pockets. In the dim glare of the parking lights, just about all the

*The Wedding Dress*

Vigg sisters could see of them was their pale hair and their blue eyes.

"We wouldn't pull a rotten trick like that," Floyd said. He added patiently, "How could anyone fake a flat tire after driving on it all night? That's a good one we've never heard before."

"You better believe it," Alvin said.

"Instead of standing here accusing innocent people of things," Floyd said, "we better think our way out of this predicament. One thing sure, we can't walk home. It's a good twenty mile and we wouldn't get home until noon tomorrow and you girls likely wouldn't make it at all. That wouldn't set too well with your pa or Alvin's and mine either. What we got to do is wait until someone comes along, flag 'em down, and borrow their tire pump. Now did any of you see anyone at the dance who could be coming home in this direction?"

"Mr. and Mrs. Kolbeinsson were there," Rosella remembered.

"They went home early," Alvin said. "They get up at three o'clock and milk their dairy cows and take the milk to town by sunup."

"Just be glad those two old gossips aren't coming past here," Doreen said. "They just go to these things to get grist for their rumor mill."

Floyd cleared his throat. "Tell you what we'll do. We'll give you girls this lantern flashlight and you can wait inside the shack. We'll stand outside with the other flash-light and flag down the first car that comes along."

They all went into the shack. The flashlight revealed a table with two chairs, an iron bedstead covered with an army blanket, and a potbellied stove with a rusted-out coffeepot sitting on it.

"This old man just disappeared off the face of the earth a year or so ago," Alvin said in an awed voice. "Been a hermit here ever since he homesteaded thirty years ago. Nobody knows what to do with this place. Maybe he'll come walking back, they say."

"Ya, Alvin, we all know that story," Floyd said.

"We'd rather sit in the car," Doreen said.

Floyd said, "Suit yourself, but I think it's fixing to rain."

A flash of lightning and an ominous roll of thunder confirmed his prediction. He grabbed a broom that was propped in a corner and swept the cobwebs off the table and chairs. The Vigg sisters tentatively sat down.

"I wish I'd brought a sweater," Rosella said, her teeth chattering. Floyd took off his suit coat and draped it over her shoulders. Alvin instantly took off his coat and draped it around Doreen. They set the lantern flashlight upright on the table, and then the Mulhallen boys started out the door to wait for help; but rain was coming down in tor-rents, and they were forced to retreat into the cabin.

"Can't even see what's coming until this is over," Floyd said. "But don't you worry, girls. We'll get you home before sunup come hell or high water."

"You'll answer to Pa if you don't," Doreen said.

"You better believe that," Alvin said grimly. "We'll wish our draft lottery numbers had come up."

The storm raged for an hour. The Vigg sisters sat frozen on their chairs, and the Mulhallen boys stood in the doorway looking out. When the rain abated at three o'clock, they went out with their flashlight and stood at the road peering for lights in the distance. Nothing but pitch dark in all directions. An owl screeched. Every half hour one of the boys came back into the cabin and said, "Don't worry. There'll be a car along any minute now."

At five o'clock dawn began to streak across the eastern horizon. The Vigg sisters had dropped their heads on the table and were dozing. Floyd said to Alvin, "I don't think anyone's coming."

Alvin said, "I think you're right, brother." He sat down on the stoop, and Floyd walked disconsolately out to the V-8. He opened and shut the doors on one side, slamming them hard. He went around to the other side, opened the front door, slammed it, then opened the other back door.

There was silence.

"Hey, Alvin. You know something? The tire pump was jammed under the backseat."

Alvin came running. "I'll be a monkey's uncle! At least our troubles are over."

"Are you kidding? This is going to make us out two dumb clods. How are we going to explain this to Pa and Martin Vigg? They'll never believe we had the tire pump in

*The Sins of the Fathers*

the car all along and we didn't find it until morning. They'll never believe that. You know they'll never believe it."

"They'll never believe it," Alvin said.

Hearing loud voices, the Vigg sisters woke up and came stumbling out to the car.

"What are you doing with that tire pump?" Doreen asked accusingly.

"We just found it," Floyd said. "It was jammed under the backseat."

"You mean it was there all the time and you never—" Rosella covered her mouth with her hand.

"Our fathers are never going to believe this," Doreen said. "Never in a hundred years are they going to believe this. You know they're never going to believe this. Never in a thousand—"

"Ya, ya," Floyd said. "Alvin and me already been through all that. I'll think up a better story when the time comes. Meantime, we got to get this tire pumped up and hit for home. Pronto."

They pumped up the tire, and Rosella got in the front seat with Floyd, and Alvin opened the back door for Doreen. "Wait a minute," she said. "Don't you think Rosella and I had better ride in the back? Pa will be upset enough without seeing we paired up."

"Nah," Floyd said, putting a restraining hand on Rosella's arm. "He'll be so mad he'll never notice."

As they started to turn onto the road, a pickup came along with an old man and woman in it. Tall milk cans were bouncing around on the truck bed. The woman stared hard at the Vigg sisters paired up with the Mulhallen boys in the new blue V-8 pulling out of the hermit's shack at sunrise, then turned her head sharply away, outraged.

Doreen rolled down her window and waved dramatically as the pickup rattled down the road. "Say good-bye to our good names," she said. "We may never see them again. Whatever happens, don't anyone in this car ever tell our fathers we ran into the Kolbeinssons this morning."

The sun was moving up brightly over the barn when the V-8 rolled up the lane of the Vigg farm. Martin Vigg was pacing the yard, followed by his dog, tail dragging and too worn out to bark. As the car came to a stop in front of him, Martin peered into the windows, his face drawn and gray.

"What have you done with my little girls?" he shouted. He pulled open the doors and started to help his daughters out, then stopped for a moment and looked from front to back and from back to front. "And you paired up partners, too!" he added bitterly.

He put his arm around each of his pale daughters, whose usually perfect curls were damp and limp, and he hugged them to him. "Oh, my poor little ones. I blame myself. I should never have let you go."

The Mulhallen boys sat stone-faced in their car, one in the front and one in the back.

"Now, Martin, I know it looks bad," Floyd said. "But we just had a round of bad luck. We ran into this thunderstorm and had to take refuge in that old homestead shack."

"The one the hermit left his furniture in?" Martin Vigg said, aghast. Then he added, "What storm?"

"A bad storm," Floyd insisted.

Martin Vigg scuffed his foot in the dirt and came up with a cloud of dust. "Didn't rain a drop here. I ought to know. I was walking my barnyard all night."

Every living thing on the Vigg farm seemed to freeze for a moment in the morning sun. A cow bawling for her calf behind the barn finally broke the silence.

"We had a flat tire," Floyd said in a dead voice. "We couldn't find the tire pump until it got light enough to see."

"Got light enough to see!" Martin Vigg's mouth fell open. "Couldn't find the tire pump until it got light enough to see? What kind of a story is that?"

"Floyd Mulhallen! I thought you were going to think up a better story than that," Doreen piped up, then gasped and clamped her hand over her mouth.

"Now you've gone and done it," Floyd roared at Doreen. "Come on, Alvin, get up front here. Our good word isn't going to be believed around here this morning, I can see that."

He revved up the V-8 and they took off, scattering chickens along the way, but Martin Vigg had the last word. "Your father will be hearing about this," he shouted.

*The Wedding Dress*

An hour after noon that same day Martin Vigg drove his truck into the barnyard of the Mulhallen place and jumped out to find Bastian Mulhallen waiting for him. They fell into each other's arms and wept hysterically.

"Oh, my dear good friend," Bastian said. "How could this terrible thing have happened to our families? But don't you worry, my boys are going to do the right thing and make honest women of your lovely daughters or my name is not Bastian Mulhallen."

Martin Vigg took a handkerchief from his back pocket and blew his nose. "What I have feared most in life has come to pass," he whispered. "The sins of the fathers are visited upon their children—both yours and mine. You know and I know, but the world must not know about this. We must work and work fast, so our children's reputations are not tarnished."

"My thinking exactly," said Bastian Mulhallen. "My boys must marry your girls by the time the month is out."

"Or maybe a little bit before," Martin Vigg said.

◆

Two weeks later the Vigg sisters and the Mulhallen boys went to the minister's house in town and were married. The minister's wife, as she always did, played Lohengrin's "Wedding March" on her piano before the vows were exchanged. The fathers had worked everything out perfectly. Doreen and Alvin would live with Martin Vigg, and Bastian would build a small house on his farm for Rosella and Floyd.

Eight months and three weeks later the Vigg sisters gave birth to seven-pound boys twenty-four hours apart. It was the kind of local story the *Little Butte Daily Gazette* loved—especially since the national news was so grim. The newspaper sent a photographer to the hospital to take pictures of the young mothers with their babies. The sisters at first protested that they didn't want their pictures taken, but the photographer wouldn't take no for an answer, and they finally relented; the babies were, after all, so beautiful.

Martin Vigg and Bastian Mulhallen stood on the sidewalk in front of the hospital shaking hands and heartily congratulating each other.

"It was close, very close, but it worked out fine," Martin said. "If you and I hadn't acted fast, though, things might have looked different."

"My thinking exactly," Bastian agreed. "And now let us go downtown and have coffee." He insisted on standing treat.

The Mulhallen boys themselves didn't know they had become fathers. They were somewhere in the South Pacific on battleships steaming toward Midway Island, and what with one thing and another going on in that part of the world, they didn't meet their sons until the little boys were almost three years old.

# 6

# Blue Horses

*One evening in August after the wheat crop has been* harvested and stored in the granary, my father pushes his chair away from the supper table and runs a hand wearily over his face. He looks at the calendar and then at my mother. "You know what time of year it is, don't you? Time for Yaccub and Elsie to drive over and try to convert us."

My father's prediction is not far off. At five the next afternoon they come roaring up the lane, the side curtains of their Model T touring car flapping ominously in the wind. They stop with a jerk in the barnyard, barely missing the windmill. Forewarned by the dog, who has heard them coming a mile away, my father and I are out waiting for them. My mother is in the house changing her apron. Bless the dog, my mother always says; he can be counted on to give her a five-minute jump on unexpected company.

Yaccub leaps from the automobile and grips my father's hand. Unfortunately, one of our horses is helping himself to a drink of water at the windmill tank, which prompts my father to make his first tactical error. "Ya, Yaccub, you old goat!" he says, pounding his old friend heartily on the back. "That horse over there brings to mind the time we painted your father's horse blue when we were kids. Recall that?"

Yaccub draws back and looks sternly at my father. "I can see you don't remember, Olaus, that the horse died. We were sinners, Olaus, sinners. 'Repent ye, therefore, and be converted, that your sins be blotted out.' Acts three, nineteen."

My father looks stunned. Two minutes into the visit and his friend has already caught him with his hands down and has landed the first punch. I know it is going to be a long night.

My mother has arrived and is helping Elsie out of the car. Elsie is a ponderous woman in a green-leaved voile dress. The Model T teeters precariously as she steps on the running board, then snaps back as she hits the ground. She has small feet and beautiful plump little hands, but after your gaze travels on up to her face and you look into her eyes, you will never remember anything else. The eyes

*The Wedding Dress*

are enormous. Round and slightly bulging, they are a diz-zyingly clear sea green, shining like two stern lamps out of her small oval face.

She and my mother shake hands somewhat formally. Elsie turns to me. "And which one of your girls is this?"

My mother replies that this is her baby, and not much of a baby anymore at thirteen. She proudly adds that the last one of her older children has just graduated from college and is out looking for a job.

"College!" Elsie moans. Her great eyes swim around full circle in her head and come to rest pityingly on my mother. "Oh, Netta, Netta, do you know that college can only make your children worldly, and being worldly they will be drawn into temptation? We are not making this mistake with Avalyn and Severin. We are going to take the twins out of school as soon as the law allows, and we will keep them home, out of the world, out of Satan's way. Even today they are at home reading their tracts."

"Come in," my mother says distractedly. "Let Olaus and Yaccub stand out here and renew old acquaintances. Has it been almost a year?"

◆

My father and Yaccub grew up together in the Red River valley. Not only did they paint horses blue together, they became drinking buddies and must have sown a bushel or two of wild oats between them in their youth. At one point, their indulgent fathers gave them money to go away to school to learn a trade, but instead they went in the opposite direction and spent it all on riotous living, ending up rafting logs in a northern Minnesota lumber camp. When western North Dakota opened up for homesteading, they came out by train to file their claims, six miles apart. Both of them sat out five long years of bachelorhood before they were able to prove up their homesteads. Mostly it was looking out of the cabin door at snowdrifts or stretches of waving prairie grass from which rocks had to be picked before the soil could be broken up for planting. My father often recalled that once he and Yaccub walked twenty miles to Little Butte to give the shoe repairman their last fifty cents to half-sole their shoes so they could walk the twenty miles back. They had promised each other that day that if they ever became rich enough to buy teams of horses they would never walk again.

Having proved up, Yaccub and my father stood up for each other at their weddings, built up their farmsteads, had children, and eventually made enough money off their wheat crops before the Dust Bowl came along to buy not only teams of horses but automobiles. The bonds between them were strong, and whenever they met in town they would duck into the saloon for a couple of beers, laughing uproariously as they regaled each other with antics of their youth. Their children played together and were baptized and confirmed together in the Norwegian Lutheran Church that stood on a windswept knoll halfway between their homesteads.

And then one day it was all over. Yaccub and Elsie went to hear a visiting evangelist at a tiny Pentecostal church on the outskirts of Little Butte called the Gospel Tabernacle of the Holy Ghost. They marched up to the altar, threw themselves on the floor and renounced "the world and all its wicked ways," and would never have anything to do with us again, except for their yearly visits to try and convert us.

Not only were the good times for the two families over, but Yaccub and Elsie's conversion was a source of frequent arguments between my mother and father. My mother strongly approved of the conversion because Yaccub had taken the pledge. She always pointed out that Yaccub had been known to go on drunken binges, and anything that turned him permanently sober was all right with her. If my mother had been born twenty years earlier, she would have been a great disciple of Carry Nation, gladly following the fiery temperance leader with an axe to wreck every saloon in sight. My father said that a convivial drink or two was good for the soul as well as the body, and he grieved for the loss of his friend.

"Yaccub is not sociable anymore," he complained. "And what about his family? Elsie is even more of a holy roller than Yaccub, and she is making hermits out of Avalyn and Severin. Thank God the older children left home and got clear away before they got converted, too. Children should not have to sit home indoors all day reading tracts."

My mother would never say a word against Yaccub and

Elsie. When they came for their yearly visit she treated them royally, always cooking up *rømmegrøt*, their favorite Norwegian porridge, and she would listen patiently to their exhortations hour after hour, on into the night.

A week before their present visit, however, my father noticed a disturbing item in the *Little Butte Daily Gazette,* which created even more friction between him and my mother. The weekly police record listed one Yaccub Trigg as having been arrested for drunk driving. An even more distressing item followed a couple of days later. It was a one-sentence letter to the editor: *Dear Sir: I wish to make it clear that I am not the Yaccub Trigg who was arrested for drunk driving Wednesday a week.* (Signed) Yaccub Trigg.

"I bet you all the cheeses in Denmark," my father said, "that there are not two men named Yaccub Trigg in this whole blamed county, or even in the state of North Dakota, when it comes to that.

"Do you know that Yaccub is not even a real name?" my father went on. "Yaccub himself has told me I don't know how many times that his name was supposed to be Jacob, but his father didn't know how to spell it when he went to the courthouse to fill out the birth certificate, so he spelled it the way it sounds in Norwegian."

"I don't care a thing about that," my mother countered. "If Yaccub says that drunk wasn't him, you can bet on that. And you can keep your Danish cheeses—wherever it is you keep them."

I had often wondered myself why my father was always betting all the cheeses in Denmark. We were one hundred percent Norwegian, and I had never seen a Danish cheese. Nevertheless, the cheeses along with Yaccub's letter had been tossed back and forth furiously between my parents for three days before Yaccub and Elsie drove in.

❖

"Go right on in," my mother says, opening the screen door wide for Elsie. "Do you know I'm going to make you *rømmegrøt* for supper?"

She settles Elsie cozily in a kitchen chair near the cookstove, where they can talk while my mother makes the porridge. We can be thankful for one thing, my father always said; Yaccub and Elsie didn't give up their hankering for Norwegian food when they got converted. Which is about all they didn't give up, he would add bitterly.

My mother goes into the pantry and brings out a saucepan full of milk and a large frying pan filled with heavy sour cream. She pushes the milk to the back of the stove and sets the cream on the hot part of the stove to boil until it has been reduced by half. Elsie and I watch as she sifts flour over the boiling cream, knowing that in a few minutes the butter will begin to bubble out. The cream thickens, and my mother stirs vigorously.

"Oh, Netta, Netta," Elsie says. "Rejoice, rejoice with us because our Avalyn has spoken in tongues!"

My mother's spoon stops for a moment its frantic journey around the frying pan. "Oh?" my mother says. Her face, already red from the heat of the stove, grows redder. She hands me a gravy spoon and begins to tilt the pan so I can ladle the drawn butter into a pitcher.

"It was four weeks ago Sunday night," Elsie says, her voice becoming husky. "We were coming home from prayer meeting around midnight and just as we got past that curve in the road where you can see the butte looming up on the horizon, a sudden gust of wind shook the car. There was a flash of lightning and great rolling thunder, and Yaccub could scarcely keep the car on the road, and the side curtains were trying to blow off, and that is when Avalyn started to speak in tongues!"

Elsie is moaning now, and her sea green eyes are bulging and glittering and rolling. "The Holy Ghost came through those side curtains and set upon her as a cloven tongue of fire. She fell back on the seat and began to speak in tongues you have never heard or will again. Oh, that child will never be the same, Netta!"

Transfixed, I stare at Elsie, and I imagine Avalyn, who is my age but whom I haven't seen for years, as a little girl with green eyes and golden curls struggling on the backseat of the Model T with the Holy Ghost as fire curls from her mouth. My legs go weak and the kitchen starts whirling round and round, and I clutch at my mother's sleeve. She looks at me sharply, puts her arm around my waist, pushes the pan to the back of the stove, and propels me out of the door.

*The Wedding Dress*

"It's nothing," I say. "I just got a little dizzy from the heat."

My mother sets me down on the edge of the porch. She mops my forehead with her apron. "You must not listen to any more of this," she whispers. "You sit here now and don't move until I call supper. If you hear anything more, you put your hands over your ears."

My head begins to clear, and then I hear Elsie's voice break into a sob. "We have all, all of our small remaining family, spoken in tongues now." I quickly clamp my hands over my ears and move to the other end of the porch.

I see my father and Yaccub behind the barn looking at the cows. My father is gesturing with a sweep of his arm toward the pastures, and I hope he isn't saying anything more about painting horses blue. I close my eyes, and when I open them the men are walking toward the house. As they pass Yaccub's automobile and come closer I can pick up their voices.

"You having trouble getting parts for that Model T, Yaccub? Old Henry stopped making it in '27."

"The Lord provides."

"If He quits coming through, I got my old T sitting in my machine shed you're welcome to take the parts off. I drove a Model A straight through the drought years. When the rains started coming back last year I traded it in for a secondhand V-8."

As Yaccub starts to say, "Gather not up for yourselves

treasure on earth—" my mother drowns him out by calling "Supper!" in a high bright voice.

The men come in and hang their hats on the kitchen wall. Yaccub is a thin slight man with high cheekbones and keen deep-set eyes, which my father says give him the look of a fox. He has lost most of his hair. What is left is reddish gray and bristles out from behind his ears.

My mother motions everyone to the table. I see that she has finished making the *rømmegrøt* and has poured the creamy porridge on five dinner plates and set them around the table, along with tall glasses of milk. The porridge has been sprinkled with sugar and cinnamon and is rimmed with the golden drawn butter.

We sit down and Yaccub prays. "Oh, dear Jesus, we are here tonight to bring straying lambs into the flock. All we like sheep have gone astray. Let your light so shine before men that they will see the error of their way and forsake all worldliness . . ."

I open my eyes and steal a look at my father. His eyes are wide open, and he is staring balefully into his cooling porridge.

"Get thee behind us, Satan. Do not let us covet material things that will lead us into temptation. Not put everything on our backs nor covet what is on our neighbors' backs. Oh, let us retreat from the world and live in solitude and read our tracts to the glory of your Holy Name. Bless this house, and before we leave here this night help us to bring these lost sheep into your corrals forever and ever, Amen."

We all pick up our spoons and start to eat. The late afternoon sun, streaming through the double windows behind the table, glints on the drawn butter rimming our plates, and they shine like gold. Nothing is heard for a few minutes except the spoons clicking on the plates. Then Yaccub looks fiercely into my mother's eyes and says, "You are the best *rømmegrøt* maker this side of Bergen!"

"He dares to say that," Elsie says, "because I have never got the hang of it. The Lord himself knows it isn't because I haven't tried."

Yaccub looks at his wife kindly. "Ya, the Lord knows *that* for a certainty!"

After supper Yaccub insists on going out with my father to help milk the cows, and Elsie says firmly that she will help wash the dishes. This fills me with foreboding. It is a sure sign they plan to make a night of it. My mother pulls a chair in front of the cookstove, where Elsie can sit with a dish towel and dry the dishes as my mother puts them in the rinse pan. I run back and forth from stove to cupboard putting the dried dishes away. My father and Yaccub come in carrying the pail of cream. They have separated the milk in the separator room in the barn and have put the skimmed milk in the trough for the pigs. My mother stores the cream in the pantry, and then we all go out on the porch to watch the sun go down.

*Here it comes now,* I think, a shiver running down my

spine. The hours of praying and exhorting and pleading throughout the night.

The grownups sit in the rockers and I sit on the porch floor, swinging my legs off the edge. The porch faces north. Far off in three directions are amber fields where the wheat has just been taken off. The sun, slowly gliding toward the horizon, picks up the amber and turns it to gold. It reminds me of the drawn butter we have just eaten. Acres and acres of drawn butter.

"Let us pray," Yaccub says.

"Hallelujah," Elsie whispers fervently, clasping her hands and bowing her head. I look at my parents. My father has his arms crossed over his chest and his legs spread straight out in front of him as he stares impassively out over his fields. My mother's face has broken up a little as if she might at any moment cry.

"It is not for us to know the times nor the seasons," Yaccub intones. "But the sun shall be turned into darkness and the moon into blood before the great and notable day of the Lord shall come. And it shall come to pass, that whosoever shall call on the name of the Lord shall be saved. Oh friends that sit here with us today, save yourselves from this untoward generation. Be born again and come into wondrous glory forever and ever, amen."

"Amen!" Elsie echoes, rocking back and forth in ecstacy.

My father unfolds his arms and takes a deep breath, as though he has just stopped after running a great distance.

*The Wedding Dress*

"We are not heathens," he says, to no one in particular.

"But Brother Olaus," Yaccub answers vehemently. "Are you committed? Have you *given* yourself? Have you renounced this wicked world and all its ways?"

"I have been baptized and confirmed. Have you forgotten that day you and I were confirmed together down in the Red River valley?" my father asks. "All my children, too. You know as well as I do. Yours and mine together. I go to church down the road here every Sunday. I'm honest. I don't cheat my neighbor. When I die I hope I go to heaven. But if I do not, I don't suppose I will know about it anyway. I don't believe I'm going to burn in hell, when it comes to that."

"Not believe in hell!" Yaccub exclaims incredulously.

"Oh, you poor soul," Elsie whispers.

"If you don't believe in hell you don't believe in the Devil, either," Yaccub shouts, "and the Devil is in fact pounding at your door day and night so that he can get in your house and lead you out into temptation. Oh, Brother Olaus, you need more help than even I had ever imagined."

"Repent!" Elsie commands, fixing my father with eyes that flash like pale emeralds in the glancing rays of the sun.

"I'm going to make coffee," my mother says abruptly. "Why don't you come in the house with me, Elsie?"

I follow them into the kitchen, but when Elsie settles herself on her chair and says, "Netta, did I ever tell you about the time Severin spoke in tongues? It was a year ago last Pentecost . . ." my mother looks hard at me, and I retreat to the porch.

The locusts have started to sing, and the men are sitting silently, each seemingly absorbed in his own thoughts. Soon Yaccub clears his throat and hitches his rocker closer to my father's. "My wife does not read the newspaper," he says in a strangely low voice. "She thinks it is too worldly."

"Ya?" my father replies.

"I suppose you saw that business in the paper last week," Yaccub continues in the same low voice.

"Ya, sure, I saw it," my father says.

"What did you think?"

"I thought it must have been your letter that was printed. If it wasn't yours, there are three Yaccub Triggs running around in this territory somewhere, and that would be hard to believe."

Yaccub turns his head sharply. "Three?" he asks in a thin voice.

"It would have to be three if you didn't write the letter," my father answers matter-of-factly. "If some other Yaccub Trigg wrote it, that makes one. You make two, of course. And the other Yaccub Trigg I know—the one who was arrested—would make three."

"You know this . . . Yaccub Trigg who was arrested?"

"Ya, sure I do. I see him walking around in town. You have maybe seen him too and didn't know him. We spent some time in saloons together in the old days, him and I. A heck of a nice fellow. He is apt to go on a bender once in a while. I have never held that against him."

Yaccub jumps up from his chair, agitated, and starts to pace the length of the porch. He stops and stares at my father. The last crimson rays of the sun still clinging to the horizon are bright on his face. A moment later the sun drops as if someone below has jerked it, and Yaccub's face is thrown into shadow. He turns and shouts into the house. "Elsie! It is late. Time to go home!"

Standing outside in the dusk we listen to the Model T roaring down the road, then fading into the distance. My mother wrings her hands and fusses about why Yaccub and Elsie have gone home so early. "I have never known them to go home until well after midnight," she says. "What went wrong?"

My father is silent. She turns to me. "You were out here. Tell me what happened."

I look at my father. He is standing with his hands jammed into his pockets, looking up at the windmill. A gentle breeze has blown up and the wheel is going around slowly, making a soft chink-chinking sound with every revolution as the water is lifted from the well. He looks so sad I think I am going to cry.

"I don't know," I blurt. "I was looking for lightning bugs."

My mother looks at me suspiciously. "You know good and well lightning bugs don't show up until after dark."

She turns to my father. "That letter in the newspaper didn't come up, did it?"

My father is still squinting up at the windmill. "It came up."

"I was right, wasn't I?" my mother asks. "That drunk wasn't our Yaccub."

My father's head comes down, and he looks straight into my mother's eyes.

"You were right," he says. "It was another man with the same name after all."

*The Wedding Dress*

# 7

# Twilight and June

*Twilight Smith could always depend on Pete* Hanson, his neighbor on the adjoining farm, to drive over in his pickup truck and ply him with all the news he didn't want to hear. When Pete drove in one crisp April morning to inform him that Twilight's longtime girlfriend June Ness had driven off the day before, straight from the school-house where she was teaching, and married Ralph Solveig, a farmer from the next township, Twilight opened his cupboard and smashed to the floor every cup on the shelf. It was not as bad as it sounded, because none of the cups had handles on them, and in any case Twilight stopped short of reaching up to the high shelf where his mother's fine bone china was stored.

Twilight swore to God he would never go with another woman—in particular a Norsky woman. The next day he threw into a grocery box and sent back by parcel post every gift he could lay his hands on, no matter how used up or ragged, that June had given him over the years. He rounded up three black leather mackinaws, one her last year's Christmas present, which he was still wearing. He hated to give that one up because it was good and warm. But it would be like ice on his shoulders now. The other two had been worn to shreds, and the cats were sleeping on them. They went in the box, too, along with a pair of boots that had leaked the day she gave them to him. A telephone address book. Boy, that was a joke; you had to drive thirty miles into Little Butte to find a telephone, and then the only people you could call were right there. Someone must have given it to *her,* and she wanted to get rid of it. The heavy silver pocket watch he had carried for years. It could be the one thing, he reflected as he untied it from the worn leather strap on his watch pocket, that in an uncommon burst of generosity she might have laid out a little money for. A western turquoise pinky ring. Imagine Twilight Smith, all two hundred and twenty-five pounds of him, in a pinky ring. Besides, it was maybe five sizes too small. A nine by twelve framed picture of herself he had sitting on his mother's Clarendon upright piano. The only object in his house he ever dusted. He took one last look at it. A pasty faced, snub-nosed woman with pale eyes and pale hair waved close to her head stared fixedly back at him. You had to hand it to these Norsky women, he thought grudgingly; they were lookers, no matter what else you had to say about them. Bam! The picture landed face down in the box.

A week after he had mailed the box he found an envelope in the mailbox with their engagement ring in it wadded up in tissue paper. This enraged him. A valuable thing like that. He had spent years paying for it on time from the skimpy sale of his wheat crops in Dust Bowl years that were bad one year and worse the next. And now the ring wasn't worth more than a three-cent stamp to her. It might have got lost in the mail for all that, and he would never have known the difference. His first impulse had been to throw it in the kitchen stove, burn it into nothing but a crusty circle. But his Scottish blood rebelled in him at the last moment, and finally he took it, still wadded in the tissue paper, to Little Butte and put it into his safety deposit box at the bank. He vowed he would never look at it again. When he died, his heirs, if he ever had any— which was doubtful considering recent events—could do with it what they wanted.

He had just come out of the bank and was walking down the sidewalk trying to keep his cap on in a stiff northwest wind which had suddenly blown up, when he saw June and Ralph walking toward him. He didn't recognize June at first because she was wearing a red dress and a snug little red hat with a veil. He had never known her to wear red; she had always stuck to pale clothes to match her hair. She was clinging to Ralph's arm as though he were the prize of all time or something. They had a mean-looking yellow hound trailing after them. Twilight blanked out for a moment, as if someone had shone a bright light in his face. He turned blindly and walked out into the middle of the street, the tumbleweeds whirling past him. Then he heard the hound barking angrily and coming after him. He stepped into the swinging doors of the Diamond Rail just as the dog made a grab for his trouser leg and missed. As he staggered to the bar he heard June's high laughter rippling down the street with the wind.

He drank two glasses of whiskey, drove the thirty miles home in thirty minutes in the forty-mile-an-hour gale, then sat in his father's old rocker and raged. How could he have been so thickheaded? *Twilight and June. Twilight and June.* The two of them must have set the record for the longest engagement in the history of the territory. He totted up the years in his head. *Nine!* It had started the year his parents had packed up and moved back to Pennsylvania. The move had been Twilight's idea. The day he turned twenty-one he sat with his parents at the kitchen table and said, "Look, you two. There isn't a day since you came to North Dakota to homestead that you haven't wished you were back East. Why don't you go, and I'll stay here and farm and send your share of the crops. Go back, while there's still time, to your house with that picket fence you're always talking about!"

The truth was that he had been good and sick of hearing his mother talk about that picket fence; there was scarcely a day when he was growing up that his mother hadn't talked about it. She would look out of the windows of their farmhouse at the prairie rolling to the horizon in every direction, and she'd say, "Oh, if we only had a little picket fence around this house like we have in Pennsylvania!" Then she'd give a huge quivering sigh and wonder if the tenants were keeping it painted. His father would slap his knee and laugh out loud as if he didn't give a hang about the picket fence and then say offhand, "But I wouldn't mind seeing them mountains again."

So they went, and his mother left him everything in the house she couldn't get in a suitcase, including her bone china. "One of these days, Twilight," she said, "you'll want to get married, maybe to that nice June Ness up the road, if she'll have you, and she's more likely to have you if you have some nice things to start out with."

That was the only thing he'd ever taken her advice about: that nice June Ness up the road. Because he already had his eye on her long before his mother mentioned it. For nine years he had waited on her every move. Anywhere she wanted to go he was there to drive her. At every country school she ever taught, whether it was in this township or the next, he had come for her each Friday night and taken her home to her parents, who lived on the farm a mile down the road from him. Once he had come to school on his tractor to get her, the only vehicle he had on the place that would negotiate the muddy ruts in the road after a sudden spring thaw. She had looked out of the schoolhouse window at the tractor and chirped in that trembly voice of hers, "I see your gallant steed awaits my pleasure, Twilight."

He had picked up on it, and every time he came for her after that, in whatever he happened to be driving on four wheels, he always said, "My gallant steed awaits your pleasure!"

He had escorted her to church suppers, Ladies Aids, wedding dances, had taken her thirty miles to Little Butte to the movies, and always she had held him at arm's length. Thanks, Twilight, she'd say as he dropped her off at the door, and she'd double up her fist and punch him on the arm and laugh up at him, and that was supposed to be thanks enough for him. He thought back to all of the times he'd said wasn't it about time they got married, and she had answered, "Just a little longer, Twilight, I've got things to do first."

The main thing, it turned out, that she had to do first was to wait for another man to come along. He had been the spare all of these years, like a sturdy old suit coat hanging in the closet that would make do in a pinch.

He didn't know Ralph Solveig all that well, but he knew *of* him. And if this was the man June had dropped him for, it didn't say much for Twilight Smith. Not that Ralph was a bad-looking man, if it came to that. He was slight, not much taller than June, with a thin face and a whole lot of dark hair he was always slicking back with his pocket comb. But he was shifty eyed, would never look a man straight on. Money ran through his fingers like dry silt. His parents had left him a good quarter-section of homestead land, free and clear, and in just a few years Ralph had mortgaged it to the hilt. He was always one step ahead of the American State Bank and foreclosure. It wasn't that he drank or chased women out of the ordinary or anything like that. He just seemed to be one of those men who had things drop out from under them. He always planted too early or too late, his seed rotted in the ground or dried up, and if anyone was hailed out, it always seemed to be Ralph Solveig. His neighbors said, "Never drive past the Solveig place. Bad luck is liable to tail you home!" His buildings were in various stages of disintegration, as if an earthquake had hit each one on schedule. His rusted-out machinery stood helter-skelter like pockmarks between them.

Of course Ralph Solveig *was* Norsky. He had that going for him as did about a hundred and ten percent of the farmers in the territory, but Twilight refused to believe that his own Scottish ancestry had anything to do with June's rejection. If it came to that, he could trace his ancestry back to the Declaration of Independence. Just because his parents had traveled from Pennsylvania to homestead on the western plains instead of coming from some unpronounceable place in Norway, it couldn't, it seemed to Twilight, be held against him.

❖

After tormented days and sleepless nights trying to sort things out in his head, he knew he was going to have to get a hold on himself or lose his mind. The best way to forget, he decided, was to never see June or Ralph again. And for a few months this was easy, because they lived on Ralph's place in the next township, where Twilight never had any business anyway. But then, one right after the other, June's parents died and left June the farm. She and Ralph lost no time in selling Ralph's place for what they could get for it to pay off the mortgages, and then they moved to the old Ness place. Just like that—there they were—his neighbors. It became almost a full-time occupation for Twilight to avoid running into them. Both the Ness farm and Twilight's sat up against the only graded country road going into Slope, the small town five miles down the road where he hauled his grain to the elevator and did all of his trading. There was scarcely a day he didn't go to Slope. Now, to avoid driving past the Ness place, he had to turn in the opposite direction and make a little jog onto an unimproved township road and drive three miles around the section before he again hit the road going to Slope. The heavily rutted roads shook the daylights out of him and beat up his truck tires.

In no time at all the old Ness place began going to wrack

and ruin under Ralph's hand. Even a mile away Twilight could see it. One night in the summer of 1941 a small cyclone came through and caved in half of the barn roof. Ralph just left it there; he moved the cows over to the other side of the barn. That summer Twilight and Pete Hanson and his other neighbors had their first bumper crop after a decade of drought. They were walking around with money jingling in their pockets from the sale of thirty-bushel-to-the-acre wheat and celebrating in every saloon along the way as they went to the courthouse to pay back property taxes that the state of North Dakota had declared a moratorium on in the Dust Bowl years. But not Ralph Solveig. His tractor had broken down at seeding time that spring, and before he got around to getting it repaired and his wheat seeded, his neighbors' crops were three inches high and bending to the wind, and the spring rains were over. A farmer had to work hard not to make any money that year, but Ralph managed to do it.

Sometimes Twilight would be out in his barnyard and would see June and Ralph driving past his place. It seemed to him they did it more often than necessary just to taunt him. They always had Ralph's dog with them. The hound would lean out of the window and bark viciously at him as they drove past. Twilight would turn his back and go in the house to sit in his father's rocker, and the rage would hit him again. Maybe he'd just sell out. Sell the damned place and go back to Pennsylvania and find his old roots. All of these Norwegians stuck together like burrs. *Blood was thicker than water.* Boy, that was the truth. But when he put his farm up for sale and was offered fifty dollars an acre less than he thought he should have received, it threw him into another kind of rage, and he vowed he'd stick it out.

◆

Strange to say about something like the war, but in a way it saved him from himself, at least bought time for him. He couldn't *wait* to enlist after Pearl Harbor, even though he could have got a farm exemption to grow his crops for the war effort. He rented out his land on crop shares to Pete Hanson, and before he knew what had hit him he was with Company C in North Africa. Went on into the Sicilian campaign and ended up slogging it all the way up the boot of Italy before it was over.

He had begged for combat duty. To have a gun in his hands. There he was, a healthy hulk of a man who had practiced marksmanship and hunted since he was fourteen, and they made him a cook. Spent the entire war in a tank destroyer battalion—cooking. Half the time he was out of baking powder. He was more in danger of being hit by his men with his own hard biscuits than by shrapnel. Once he had got hold of a couple of pounds of fresh Italian apricots and decided to surprise his men with some homemade apricot jam. He didn't put any sugar in, and they threw that back at him, too. It was the last time he tried anything fancy. When he was mustered out he still could scarcely boil water without burning it. He had made corporal and that was it. No Purple Heart for him. He had managed to get through the entire war without drawing a drop of blood, on either himself or the enemy.

Ralph Solveig, on the other hand, had more or less covered himself with glory. He, too, enlisted. He had stormed up the coast of Normandy at Omaha Beach, according to accounts in the *Little Butte Daily Gazette,* and even though wounded had pulled two of his comrades out from artillery fire. He came home not only with the Purple Heart but with the Silver Star. June was so proud of him she was ready to burst.

So then, the war was over and four years out of Twilight's life were gone, and they had diminished the rage in his head. But when he got back to his farm he still found himself driving three miles out of his way to Slope to avoid running into June and the war hero.

◆

One Saturday evening in late September, when he was on his way home from Slope and he was bone tired after hauling three loads of wheat to the elevator and already driving a total of fifteen miles out of his way, he said to himself, "This has got to stop. The hell with it." And he turned his truck down that good graded road that would get him home three miles quicker.

He thought afterward that it may have been the beer that affected his judgment, because after he had finally got his last load of wheat taken off at the elevator, which had been jammed up with trucks a half mile out of town, he had staggered wearily into the Slope bar for a couple of beers and then had crossed the street to Myra's Cafe for a bowl of her bean-and-onion stew. The stars were out by the time he headed back out into the country. They were peppering the sky low down into the horizon on all sides, and he remembered thinking to himself, "This is why I didn't move back to Pennsylvania." Right after that was when he came to the good graded road and said, "The hell with it." It was the biggest mistake he ever made.

He was bearing down on the accelerator to clear the Ness place as fast as possible when he hit a hard object in the road. His tires went *whump,* and the big truck lifted itself off the road and flipped over on its side into the ditch. His body crashed against the window on the passenger's side. The glass shattered, and he felt a piece of it pierce his thigh. He tried to get the door open above him, but he couldn't push it up in the position he was in. He cursed himself for turning on the road. He started to pull the glass from his leg but decided to leave it there. If he pulled it out he'd more than likely bleed to death. The blood was already soaking his pants. Four years in the war without a scratch, and now he was going to die on his own road he never used but once. He pushed on the door again. It wouldn't budge.

He heard the angry barking of a dog, first at a distance and then coming closer and closer. It must be that yellow hound of Ralph's. Probably better off bleeding to death in his truck than lying out on the road getting torn apart by that dog. Dogs were smart. That dog hated him.

Someone spoke to it sharply and the barking stopped. A minute later a lantern was beamed in, and Ralph Solveig's lean face peered in the window above him.

"Oh, is that you, Twilight Smith?"

*Saved by the war hero,* he thought bitterly.

"Yeah. Ran into some damn fool thing in the road. My truck flipped over on me."

"You hurt?"

"I'm okay except for a piece of glass about as big as a dinner plate stuck in my thigh."

"I'll see if I can open this door and get you out."

Ralph jerked the door open from above. He took Twilight by the shoulders and eased him out the door and over the end of the truck. Twilight fell, stiff-legged, to the ground in the glare of the headlight that had survived the crash. When he got up, the glass dropped out of his thigh and the blood streamed out of the torn place in his pants.

"Oh, my God," Ralph whispered, "I never could stand the sight of blood!" He reached into his pocket and took out a red handkerchief, stuffed it into Twilight's thigh, and held it there. The sweat began to pour off his face.

"For Christ sake, Ralph," Twilight said irritably, "how'd you ever get through the war the way you did if you can't stand the sight of blood?"

"It wasn't easy," Ralph said, and let out a short sob. He

drew in his breath and said, "Now what we got to do, see, is get a pressure bandage on this thing until we can get you to the hospital. I'm going to take my hand off now, so you put your hand on the handkerchief and press hard. I'm going to take off my shirt and tie it around your leg."

Ralph unzipped his black mackinaw, which Twilight even in his dire strait couldn't help noticing was the same kind June had given *him* for Christmas three years running. Ralph took off his red flannel shirt and got out his pocketknife and slashed off the tail. He folded the shirttail and stuffed it on top of the handkerchief in Twilight's thigh, whispering to himself that thank God the blood wouldn't show up so much through all that red cloth. He ripped off the rest of Twilight's trouser leg that hadn't been cut by the glass. He wrapped Twilight's leg with the remainder of the shirt and twisted the sleeves tightly. His hands were trembling, and his thin bare chest was dripping with perspiration.

"Now we got to get you to the hospital," he said, gasping for breath. "A good thirty mile, as you know, so I'll go home and get my pickup. June's out somewhere in her car." He put his mackinaw back on and started toward his farm on the run, whistling for his dog, who stood silently glaring at Twilight a few rods away. The dog leaped forward and growled maliciously at him before trotting after his master.

Twilight sat at the side of the road feeling the waves of blood trying to get out of his leg and looked at his truck lying on its side like a dying whale. The air was crisp and cold, already portending winter, and he began to shake. He was glad for one thing: his truck had been empty. What a mess a full load of wheat would have been.

The headlight suddenly flickered out as if the truck had died.

He heard Ralph revving up his pickup, and in a minute he was back with it. It was a sorry piece of rusted-out machinery. It sounded to Twilight as if it might be missing on one cylinder. He doubted it would get them to Little Butte.

"Hey, Ralph," he said, "why don't we just swing into my place, we're going right past, and get my pickup?"

"Naw," Ralph said, "I'm not going to load and unload you twice if I can help it. You must weigh more than ten sacks of feed tied together. We ain't got that kind of time to waste."

He helped Twilight into the truck and told him to keep his leg stretched out. They started off with a roar, and when Twilight sank back against the seat, Ralph cried out, "Hold on there now, fella, you're not going to die on me, are you? I'd never hear the last of it from June!"

"That's a good one," Twilight said. "Your wife wouldn't give the snap of her fingers whether I live or die and you know it."

"Then why is she always throwing you up to me? Every time she gets mad at me, she says, 'I could have married

Twilight Smith and lived in the lap of luxury,' and so on and on."

Twilight grunted. "Lap of luxury! Boy, that's another good one!" His leg was throbbing so fiercely he thought that any minute it would burst the bandage. He noticed that Ralph's hands on the wheel were glistening with sweat.

Ralph seemed to be having second thoughts. "What I said a few minutes ago about June," he said, "don't take it to necessarily mean we haven't had some good times."

"I can't argue with you there," Twilight said.

The pickup kept covering the miles, and Twilight kept listening to the missing cylinder, wondering if they'd make it. He ticked off the landmarks as they went past: two schoolhouses, two churches, one butte. He looked for the moon among all those stars. It was only a sliver. Not a good night for hunting. Suddenly he thought of something. He was amazed he hadn't thought of it before.

"What the heck was it I struck in your road, anyway, that made me flip over like that?"

Ralph didn't answer. Twilight looked over and saw his hands shaking on the wheel. "Did you happen to notice what it was?"

Ralph's voice was barely audible. "Could have been one of them four-by-sixes I hauled home from the lumber company this afternoon to try to jack up my barn roof. I was missing one when I got home."

It figures, Twilight thought.

*The Wedding Dress*

A great pulse in his leg shook him, and he passed out for a few minutes. When he came to, Ralph was saying, "For God's sakes don't die on me now, Twilight, we only got seven, eight more mile to go!"

"I'm not planning to cash in my chips just yet," Twilight said. "Just keep your shirt on."

"Yeah, well, I'd sure like to keep my shirt on," Ralph flared up angrily, "if it wasn't wrapped around that goddam bloody leg of yours!"

Twilight was so ashamed he was glad when he felt himself passing out again. When he woke up he was in the hospital getting a blood transfusion.

The glass had narrowly missed severing an artery. When his head cleared and he began to get his strength back he expected, all things considered, that Ralph Solveig would come in to see how he was getting along. He didn't come. Who did come, though, was a pair of teenagers he'd never laid eyes on before, carrying their schoolbooks on their hips and greeting him shyly and asking him how he was feeling now, Mr. Smith. The girl was a short little thing with red hair and pink glasses, and she smiled and smiled at him. The boy was big and had a crew cut and blinked his eyes a lot. They stood shifting their books from one hip to the other, smiling and blinking and saying they were sure glad he was coming out of it okay, Mr. Smith, until Twilight couldn't stand it any longer and said, "Look, I have a feeling this is going to turn out to be a dumb question, but am I supposed to know you two?"

They looked at each other, embarrassed, and finally the boy said, "Didn't Mr. Solveig tell you we was the ones brought you the rest of the way into Little Butte Saturday night?"

Twilight shook his head. "No, he sure didn't."

"Well, see," the boy stammered, "Linda here and me was out for a ride Saturday night after the first movie was out, and five, six mile out of town we met this man running toward us like he was crazy. Boy, was he pantin' and sweatin'. Waves us down and says he run out of gas a mile or two back and he has a hurt man in his pickup he has to get to the hospital. We took him back there to get you and brung you in. You was mostly passed out and bleedin' some."

"Out of gas, you say?" He couldn't believe it. Twilight had never known a farmer to run out of gas. The last thing a farmer did before the sun went down was to fill all the vehicles on his place with gas against the night and morning. Every farmer he ever knew had a big gas drum on his place, sitting belly down on a couple of sawhorses, and every few weeks right on schedule the Farmers Union truck would come and fill it up. Even during the war farmers got all the gas they wanted. Had to have gas to grow crops for the war effort. *Out of gas!* Ralph Solveig ran out of gas. It figured.

He shook the teenagers' hands and thanked them for saving his life. He said when he got out of the hospital maybe he'd think up some kind of reward for them. The boy turned red in the face and said, "A person shouldn't ought to be rewarded for doing what any person would of done." Twilight said he was sorry he mentioned it.

When Pete Hanson came to take him home from the hospital a few days later, Pete was bristling with news. Just once, Twilight thought wearily, just once in his life he wished Pete would bring him something he wanted to hear. The bad news was that Ralph Solveig had decided, all on his own, to get Twilight's truck out of the ditch. He had put a cable on it and had managed to get it upright, but just as he was pulling it back on the road with his tractor, the cable broke and the truck rolled over on its other side back into the ditch. Ralph had given up and left it there. Pete—always in the right place at the right time for newsmongering—had come driving by just as Ralph was leaving the scene of the crime.

"She wasn't in too bad of a shape when *you* rolled her except for all that broken glass," Pete said, "but wait'll you see her now!"

Twilight decided one thing then and there. Once he got his truck home he was going to stay off that road. Get an earlier start and drive a little faster and stay off that road.

❖

He grew old staying off that road.

Old enough so that he was thinking seriously about having himself shipped back to Pennsylvania and buried beside his parents when he died. He knew his mother and father were happy back there. They had found a cemetery with a picket fence around it. That picket fence was the one thing that kept Twilight from making the final arrangements for himself.

One day Pete Hanson, who was not so young himself anymore and never got out of his pickup for any reason except to eat and go to bed, drove over and parked in the middle of Twilight's barnyard and laid on the horn. This was the signal for Twilight to come out of his house to hear the latest portents and forebodings.

Pete rolled down his window, and his lips started moving before Twilight was halfway across the barnyard. That was fine; it gave Pete an excuse to tell his news twice. Had Twilight heard about Ralph Solveig? He'd been trying to jack up that old barn roof of his with a couple of four-by-sixes and a beam had fallen on him and killed him.

"I figure that roof blew in on him around forty years ago," Pete said. "Just about time for him to start thinking about fixing it. And I figure one of them four-by-sixes he was using was the one rolled your truck."

Twilight didn't go to the funeral. He would have felt like a fifth wheel. Even so, he would have gone if Ralph had come to see him in the hospital that time and admitted he'd run out of gas *or* if Ralph had told him that he had smashed up the other side of his truck when he tried to pull it out of the ditch. Twilight thought he might have been able to overlook one of the two misdeeds but not both of them. Of the two, though, what rankled him most, even after thirty-five years, was that Ralph had thought he was so stupid he didn't know what side his truck had flipped over on.

Anyway, he didn't have to go to the funeral to hear it. The Lutheran cemetery backed up against the far corner of his farm, and the afternoon of the funeral he could hear the Veterans of Foreign Wars putting on a big show with their drums and bugles. He could imagine June standing out there in the hot sunshine crying her eyes out as the commander gave her the American flag.

◆

When he heard what happened to June it was not, strangely enough, from Pete Hanson, but from two old women he didn't know. A couple of weeks after the funeral he had been waiting in line to buy a month's supply of groceries at the Red Owl store in Little Butte. Slope was now a ghost town, the victim of centralization and fast highways, and no longer had a grocery store or anything else for that matter, except the grain elevator standing starkly on the outskirts and about thirty residents who refused to give up.

The women were chattering in front of him and he had tuned them out—until he heard something that made his head shoot up. "I just came from the nursing home," one of them was saying. "Do you know that my good friend June Solveig is there now? It's a shame what's happened to her. Some people found her wandering around on the road one night in a daze. Not knowing what else to do with her, they took her to the home. She doesn't have anybody, you know, since Ralph died. He wasn't much, but at least he was there."

Twilight paid for his groceries and drove toward home. He turned into Pete Hanson's place and found Pete sitting in his pickup in the middle of the barnyard. Twilight pulled his own truck parallel to Pete's and called out, "Are you coming or going?"

"Neither of them two," Pete answered. "I'm just setting here waiting until the sun drops behind my cottonwood trees and it's time to go in and go to bed."

"I got a bone to pick with you," Twilight said. "Why didn't you tell me about June? You've driven over and told me about every other damn thing that's happened in this neighborhood in the last forty years, most of it I didn't want to know, so why didn't you tell me about June?"

Pete suddenly became cagey. "Well, you know, after what happened between her and you—"

"Hell!" Twilight shouted. "How bad off is she?"

"There's things she recollects and things she don't," Pete said.

The next morning, after arguing with himself all night and losing the argument, he found himself at the Lutheran Nursing Home in Little Butte asking Ida Severson at the desk what room June Solveig was in. Ida looked startled and said go on up the stairs and turn left to Ward 212. The stairs creaked under him as he climbed them. He wondered whether they made nursing homes for three hundred-pound men. He veered left and stopped in the doorway of Ward 212 and peered in. Five old ladies were sitting around in wheelchairs, all with disheveled tufts of gray hair and wearing faded bathrobes. He stared from one to the other in bewilderment. Was she one of these old ladies?

They all stared back at him, and suddenly one of them stretched out her arms and cried, "Oh, Ralph! Where have you been? I've been waiting and waiting!"

He walked blindly forward. Grasping his arms, she reached a hand up, pulled his face down, and kissed him on the cheek. "I knew you'd come! I knew it!"

She turned toward the other women and cried, "Didn't I tell you Ralph would come? Didn't I?"

One of the old ladies snickered. The others smiled a little and remained silent.

The room was a mess. Congealed leftovers from breakfast were scattered around on the bedside tables, and a bucket of water with a mop in it stood abandoned in the middle of the floor. A sixth old lady was lying in her bed in the far corner of the room breathing oxygen.

"I can't stay long today because I've got things to do back on the farm, June," he said, "but I'll be back tomorrow."

Twilight turned and walked out of the room. He went back down the creaky steps to the front desk. "Ida," he said, "I want June Solveig put into a private room, and I want her taken care of and to have everything she needs. I'll come in the first of every month and pay the bill."

He guessed that would cause some talk. *That old skinflint Twilight Smith setting up his old flame in a nursing home.* Let them talk for all he cared. Talk was cheap.

◈

He found June in her own room when he came back the next day. Her hair had been shampooed and curled. She was sitting in her wheelchair looking out of the window, down at the street below.

"I thought that was you, Ralph," she cried, "driving up in your pickup. Do you know they moved me into this nice room where I can see everyone driving past? And it's only me in here, and I don't have to listen to the complaints of all of those other ladies who are, you know, so much older than I am."

She spoke the last words with a certain coyness and put her hands to her hair and smiled at him. The years fell away, and he saw June at the schoolhouse door, looking out at his tractor. *I see your gallant steed awaits my pleasure, Twilight.*

He pulled a chair up to hers. She clung to his hand. So this was June. For the first time he dared to look at her closely. She was, after all, not so much different. She was skinny, but she had always been thin. The skin of her face was drawn delicately, almost dangerously over her bones.

Her eyes, which had always been pale, were now so

transparent it seemed he could almost see through to the back of them, except for the brown flecks, like the flecks on her hands, that spotted them. But it was her voice that startled him. It was the same high bright birdlike voice he had known. It had always been trembly. Now it was more so, bringing the memory back in full force.

She took his hand and patted it firmly. "I was sitting here thinking, Ralph, that when I get well and get out of here, why you and I are just going to fix that hole in the barn roof all by ourselves. We'll take those old four-by-sixes you've had around for so long, and we'll just raise 'em up, and—" She stared at him in horror, drew her hand away, and started to sob. He called for a nurse and left.

He stayed away for a week, until one day he heard Pete Hanson's persistent horn in the driveway. When he went out to the pickup, Pete gave him something round and heavy wrapped in newspapers. "Slice it and fry it," he said. "It'll jack you up."

Twilight smelled the package. "It's *klubb*, isn't it?" he asked suspiciously. He loved most Norwegian dishes, had probably gained a hundred pounds on them, but couldn't tolerate black pudding. The fact that it was made from pig's blood wouldn't have kept him from eating it if it hadn't given him violent indigestion.

He handed the package back. "Just give me the news straight, Pete," he said.

Pete sighed. He had run into Ida Severson that morning

on a street in Little Butte, he said, and she had asked him why Twilight wasn't coming to see June anymore.

"According to Ida, June thinks you're Ralph," Pete said. "Ida says June thinks you've deserted her, and they can't do nothing with her over there."

◆

When he walked into her room several hours later, she had her eyes glued expectantly on the door. "I was looking out the window and I knew sure as anything that was you, Ralph, when I saw your pickup pull up!"

When he sat down she grasped his hand firmly and smiled at him. "You know, when I couldn't sleep last night I was thinking that we'll leave that old barn just the way it is. We've been getting along with it fine all of these years. Why should we fuss with it? If it isn't broken, don't fix it, isn't that what you always say?" She doubled up her fist and punched him on the arm.

What Ralph had more than likely said—and what he himself had always said—was, "If it ain't broke, don't fix it." But let her have her schoolteacherish ways.

After that he came in every other day. Some days she looked uncomprehendingly at him, as if a thin curtain had dropped down over her eyes. She would sit with her hands folded tightly in her lap, staring straight ahead, and soon he would leave. She acknowledged neither his coming nor his going.

One day he walked in and her eyes were as clear as

*The Wedding Dress*

fresh rainwater. When he sat down she doubled up her fist and punched him in the arm and smiled at him before either of them had spoken.

She grabbed his hand and hung on. "I was thinking last night when I couldn't sleep what a good life you and I have had together, Ralph. All of those good years. But there are so many things I don't remember. It gives me fits sometimes, the things I don't remember I know I should remember."

She looked him straight in the eyes. "One thing I can't remember is if we had any children. Did we have children, Ralph?"

He shook his head.

"Well, I was right then. I didn't think so either."

Twilight knew what was coming next. *Why didn't we have children?* He had often wondered about that himself. But the question didn't come. She went into a long reverie, her hand twitching in his the way his dog twitched when it was dreaming. Then she came out of it and punched him. "If it isn't broken, don't fix it, isn't that what you always say, Ralph?"

He wouldn't have looked at himself in the mirror and admitted that some of the hours spent with June were the happiest hours he had spent since they broke up, but a very secret part of his brain said that this was so.

He wondered how long it could go on. Their lives seemed to be suspended on a pair of thin wires with a thread holding them together. He wondered which of the three would snap first. He tried not to think about it.

One day he walked into her room and found her unusually lighthearted. Her hair was freshly washed and her nails polished, which always put her in a good mood. She had her hands spread out in front of her, turning them this way and that, letting the fresh pink polish catch the afternoon sun that streamed through the window. The sun caught her gold wedding band, and glints of light flashed off it.

"Do you remember the day you put this on my finger, Ralph?" she asked coquettishly, twirling the band around with her other hand.

He didn't answer. A sly, secretive expression crept across her face. "I never told you, did I, that I was engaged to someone else before I met you."

She wasn't looking at him now but was gazing out of the window, lost in thought, lost in hundreds of miles and years of thoughts.

"You know, that's one of the things I can't remember. I can't remember his name."

He started to ask, thought better of it, then asked anyway. "Did—did you care for this man?"

She suddenly jerked back into the present, seized his hand, and cried remorsefully, "Oh, no, no, Ralph, I didn't care about him at all, not really, not the way I cared about you. He was just someone I went with, went *along* with, you might say, until my *prince* came along! You understand that, don't you?"

It wasn't the best day he had ever spent.

He told himself that she was crazy, out of her head, and anyone who believed a word she said was crazy too. He stayed away for three days, arguing with himself, then lost the argument again; there was enough cruelty in this world without his adding to it.

When he walked in the next afternoon, she had been watching for him from the window. She was very excited. She told him to pull up a chair. "When I saw you driving up," she said, "I suddenly remembered the name of the man I was engaged to. It was Dusk."

He took a long breath. "No, June," he replied firmly, "it was Twilight."

Her eyes clouded with confusion. She flushed, and her lips began to tremble. Suddenly her eyes flashed with anger. "What are you trying to do, Twilight," she asked sharply, "mix me up?" He got up and walked quickly out of the room.

When he came the next day he was prepared to leave at once if she was still angry. She had been looking out of the window for him, and when he walked in she smiled at him but didn't call him by name. She told him to sit down. She looked at him warily but kept smiling.

"How—how are you getting along on the farm?" she asked craftily. Twilight's throat constricted. *She's not sure who I am, but whoever I am she doesn't want to lose me.*

"Not too bad," he replied, "except I miss your cooking something fierce."

A weight seemed to fall from her shoulders. She punched him on the arm so hard he winced. "Just you wait, Ralph," she said, "when I get out of here I'll cook you up a blizzard."

He was sitting with her one cold autumn day not too long afterward when her hand suddenly twitched violently in his. She turned and looked at him. Her eyes flew open, and she chirped like a robin. She slumped forward, and her head dropped on his shoulder as he caught her. She wasn't any heavier than a sack of bird seed. He rocked her back and forth in his arms. As he rocked he looked out of the window and saw his pickup, sprinkled with snow, parked at the curb. *Your gallant steed awaits my pleasure, Twilight.* It occurred to him that he should call someone, but there wasn't anything anyone could do. He kept rocking until he heard the supper carts coming at the far end of the corridor, and then he pressed the button to summon a nurse.

◆

He had her buried beside Ralph in the Lutheran cemetery behind his farm. Ralph already had the small military headstone from the army, but she didn't have anything. He let it go for a while, but she didn't have anyone else to do it for her, and Ralph didn't have any next of kin, either. Neither did he himself, when it came to that. He went to the Monument Company in Little Butte one day and leafed through the catalog. He came on one particular stone that was so silly it made him smile, and then he quickly passed it by and looked through the remainder of the book. He paged back and forth, always coming back to the one that made him smile. It really tickled him, made him feel almost lighthearted. It was a tall, narrow red limestone which had vines sculpted at the top in an arc. Over the arc were two chubby angels flying together, holding hands. Under the arc were engraved the words TOGETHER FOREVER.

June would be *crazy* about that stone. He didn't know about Ralph, but Ralph wasn't going to have any choice in the matter. He ordered the stone made up to read:

RALPH SOLVEIG
1914–1982
JUNE NESS SOLVEIG
1913–1982

While he was at it, he had his own gravestone erected. He'd given it some thought. He'd thrown in his lot with the Norskies since before he could remember; he might as well go the distance with them. His plot was parallel to June and Ralph's, about twenty feet away. His stone was

white, the same size as theirs, but it didn't have any curli-
cues on it. It read:

TWILIGHT SMITH
1912–